"I should never have let

Neither should he, Dallas
straight."

"I'm not that tipsy," Paris said, her speech slurred. "I came here to convince you to hire me, not to make out with you."

"It was just a kiss, Paris. And I'm the one who should've stopped it."

Paris dropped down onto the mattress. "I'm not... normally...like this." She followed the comment with a hiccup and a giggle.

"You've got a good excuse. Now lie down and sleep it off."

"Thank you, Dallas Calloway. You're a nice man. I'm sorry I'm not acting like a nice girl."

"No need to apologize."

She sent him a sleepy smile. "Since I probably blew my chances at the job, I wouldn't mind a kiss goodnight."

He might have laughed if he hadn't been so damn tempted.

* * *

The Rancher's Marriage Pact is part of the Texas Extreme series: Six rich and sexy cowboy brothers live—and love—to the extreme!

Dear Reader,

Fifteen years ago, I began my journey as a published author with *Cowboy For Keeps,* a book set in Texas, which seemed logical given I'm a born and bred fourth-generation Texan. Since that time, I have traveled to many places in my stories, from the fictional Middle East to Cypress to Las Vegas and several points in between. I have featured heroes who are doctors, lawyers, lawmen and royals, and I've enjoyed each and every one.

But a few months ago, I felt compelled to return to my roots with Texas Extreme, a South Texas series set on a large working cattle ranch and featuring six sexy, thrill-seeking men with a dash of family scandal thrown in for good measure. After all, I have actually lived on a ranch, been to more rodeos than I can count and have an abiding respect for cowboys, so why not join all three? That's exactly what I've done with the Calloway brothers and the women who attempt to corral them into commitment.

First up—Dallas Calloway, the eldest brother who likes to be in control and can charm a girl right out of her bloomers. He has no intention of settling down, but then there is this little issue with a will...and a woman he can't seem to resist.

I truly hope you enjoy the first installment of Texas Extreme. Just remember to hang on to your hats because it's going to be a wild ride!

Happy reading!

Kristi

THE RANCHER'S MARRIAGE PACT

KRISTI GOLD

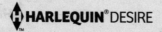

H HARLEQUIN DESIRE

Recycling programs
for this product may
not exist in your area.

ISBN-13: 978-0-373-73448-1

The Rancher's Marriage Pact

Copyright © 2016 by Kristi Goldberg

Printed in U.S.A.

Kristi Gold has a fondness for beaches, baseball and bridal reality shows. She firmly believes that love has remarkable healing powers, and she feels very fortunate to be able to weave stories of love and commitment. As a bestselling author, a National Readers' Choice Award winner and a Romance Writers of America three-time RITA® Award finalist, Kristi has learned that although accolades are wonderful, the most cherished rewards come from networking with readers. She can be reached through her website at kristigold.com, or through Facebook.

Books by Kristi Gold

Harlequin Desire

The Return of the Sheikh
One Night with the Sheikh
From Single Mom to Secret Heiress
The Sheikh's Son
One Hot Desert Night
The Sheikh's Secret Heir

Texas Extreme

The Rancher's Marriage Pact

Visit the Author Profile page at Harlequin.com, or kristigold.com, for more titles!

To my childhood companion,
very best friend and surrogate sister,
Charlotte L.

One

The Last Chance Ranch...

Her first thought, as she left her compact sedan and strode toward the single-story white stone structure set somewhere between San Antonio and the middle of nowhere. Her second thought—the South Texas weather was ridiculously hot for March. She should never have worn the tailored black blazer and skirt. Fortunately she'd twisted her hair up and off her neck that was now damp with perspiration. Of course in part, her current predicament could be attributed to nerves, not the afternoon sun. And a good dose of desperation.

Once she reached the threshold, Paris flipped her sunglasses up onto her head and noted the wooden plaque to the right of the entry.

"Welcome to the D Bar C, where cowboys and hospitality rule. Take off your boots, hang your hat and come in to sit a spell. And if we don't happen to be here, just reach out and ring the bell."

Cute. Very cute. Unfortunately she wasn't wearing a hat or boots, but what she wouldn't give to kick off her three-inch heels and barrel in barefoot. Not a banner idea when applying for a job, and boy did she need this job. Of course, the position hadn't exactly been announced, yet that hadn't stopped her from showing up, uninvited, which could result in rejection. Nothing new there.

After smoothing a palm down her jacket, Paris drew in a calming breath as she clutched the strap of the teal briefcase hanging from her shoulder. She exhaled slowly before opening the heavy mahogany door to find the place blessedly cool, otherwise she might have shed her blazer to reveal the sheer sleeveless white shell. The area happened to be completely deserted, not one soul in sight behind the lengthy mahogany counter, yet she did spot the aforementioned bell.

She could ring it to summon someone, or she could wait. She could leave, or she could convene some courage and see this through. But she had come too far to give up now.

In a fit of sheer procrastination, Paris took a few moments to study the area with a designer's eye. Aside from the usual office equipment behind the counter, she discovered typical Western decor—burnt-orange-and-white cowhide chairs set about the waiting area, massive stone fireplace with a heavy wood mantel, a set of horns hanging above said mantel. She moved closer to read the bronze plaque below the sad symbol of human cruelty to find it etched with "Prize twelve-point buck bagged by J. D. Calloway."

Lovely. Just lovely. She supposed she should be thankful dear J.D. had only saved the horns as a souvenir and not the poor deer's entire head.

More than ready to see this spontaneous plan through, Paris turned back to the counter and reached for the bell with a trembling hand. But before she could pick it up, a tall, dark-haired man emerged from an entry at the far end of the office, looking as if he had walked right out of an Old West time warp and into the future. He kept his attention trained on a document clasped in his rather large and masculine hands as he strode toward her, the jingle of spurs echoing against the beige walls, providing her the prime opportunity to do a comprehensive inspection. He was every bit a cowboy, from the top of his tan hat to the tip of his brown leather boots. He wore a faded blue shirt and equally faded blue jeans, yet the large silver belt buckle drew her immediate focus. She noticed the word *Champion* before her gaze traveled lower to a place no self-respecting, professional woman should go.

"Can I help you, ma'am?"

At the sound of the incredibly deep voice, Paris's attention returned to the cowboy's face, her cheeks flaming from mortification. "Uh, actually, I'm…" Heavens, the impact of his silver-blue eyes caused her to forget her name. She'd seen several photographs of him, yet none had done Dallas Calloway justice.

He reacted to her momentary mental lapse with a

half smile, revealing a deep dimple creasing the left of his whisker-shaded jaw. "Are you lost?"

"Not really," she managed to say although in a sense she did feel a bit lost. "I'm Paris Reynolds."

He leaned over the counter and offered a hand. "Dallas Calloway. What can I do for you?"

That question was as loaded as a shotgun. But since this man could hold the key to her future financial security, she had to regain her composure. "I'm here about your new venture."

Before he could respond, a petite woman dressed in a plain tailored floral blouse covering faded jeans, her silver-and-brown hair twisted into a braid, strode into the room and pulled up short when she caught sight of the pair. She eyed Paris with suspicion as she made her way to Dallas's side. "Whatever you're selling, we're not buying."

Paris had the feeling no one crossed this woman and lived to tell about it. "I'm not selling anything but my services."

She huffed. "For your information, my stepson doesn't have to pay for it."

When awareness dawned, another bout of embarrassment plagued Paris. "You've definitely misunderstood my motives. I'm here to discuss a *business* proposition." Not that the explanation sounded much better, evidenced by the woman's raised eyebrows.

"Stop jumping to conclusions, Mom," Dallas interjected. "I'm fairly sure that's not what she's selling."

The woman propped a hand on her hip and sneered.

"Dallas deals on a daily basis with females who come here under the guise of business."

"Oh, so true, Maria," came from behind Paris. "Our stepson is a regular chick magnet."

Paris turned to find a pretty middle-aged blonde dressed in a chic coral sundress, standing at the front door. Apparently the place was rife with the now-deceased J. D. Calloway's wives. Determined to get off on the right foot with this one, she held out her hand and smiled. "I'm Paris Reynolds."

The blonde returned her smile and shook her hand with much more gusto than Paris expected. "I'm Jenny Parks Calloway, J.D.'s third wife."

"Not officially," Maria added in a sour tone.

Paris assumed there must be a story behind that comment, but chose to remain silent and await the fallout between the feuding former spouses.

It came out in Jenny's intense frown. "Please forgive the second missus. Sometimes Maria forgets her manners. What shade on the color chart is your blond, if you don't mind me asking?"

Paris's hand immediately went to her hair. "I wouldn't know. I'm actually a natural blonde."

Jenny chuckled. "Oh, so am I."

"And I'm the queen of Texas," Maria said with a smirk.

Ignoring the other mother, Jenny turned her smile back on Paris. "By the way, I love, love, love your suit, sugar."

Paris grasped to find a return compliment. "Thank you, and I love your bracelet."

Jenny twisted the diamond and silver leaf bauble around her wrist. "And thank you. I picked this up at a silent auction at the art center in San Antonio last month."

Unbelievable. "Really? I was there, too." But she hadn't had the funds to bid. She'd been there to drum up business. An unsuccessful plan that had led her to this remote ranch.

Jenny laid a hand beneath the strand of pearls at her throat. "A small, small world it is."

"Way too small if you ask me," Maria grumbled.

Jenny sent her another scowl. "No one asked you, Maria, and no one appreciates your attitude or your sarcasm. You really should learn some Southern decorum."

"I think we all can work on that," Dallas chimed in as he opened the half door built into the counter. "Ms. Reynolds, if you'll follow me to my office, we can get away from all this verbal sparring and you can tell me what you need."

"But make it quick," Maria added. "He has work to do."

"Oh, hush," Jenny replied as Paris stepped through the opening. "He's not too busy to entertain a pretty girl. Also, their names go so well together—Paris and Dallas. Sounds like a match made in heaven."

"Sounds like an airport flight schedule," Maria muttered.

"It's high time he meets a nice girl, Maria," Jenny added. "Don't forget what's coming up at the end of the week and we both know what that means."

If only Paris knew what that meant. Regardless, she

could tell Dallas wasn't comfortable with the conversation when he rushed toward an opening to his left without responding.

With her mind riddled with confusion, Paris followed Dallas down a lengthy corridor, all the while unsuccessfully trying to keep her eyes off his derriere. She found the way he dangled his arms at his sides, his perfect lean build and the roll of his hips quite fascinating.

Good grief. Evidently the lengthy amount of time she'd been without male companionship had her falling head over common sense over some cowboy. Okay, not just any cowboy. An extremely gorgeous, rich cowboy who had succeeded at everything he'd tried, from rodeo to ranching, according to what she'd read on the internet. A far cry from her seedy ex-husband who'd managed to screw up everything he'd endeavored, including their marriage.

Dallas soon paused to lead Paris into a well-appointed office that served as a tribute to his success. The lush brown leather sofa and love seat set near the window complemented his masculine aura, and the massive mahogany desk spoke to his rugged persona. The hand-scraped dark wood floors topped off the decor that couldn't have been done any better if she'd done it herself, even if it wasn't exactly her cup of tea.

"Would you like something to drink?" he asked as he crossed the room to the elaborate granite-covered wet bar in the corner.

"Water would be fine," she said, *although wine would be better*, she thought.

"Water it is. Have a seat."

After settling in a beige club chair across from the desk, Paris set her case on the floor, crossed her legs, adjusted her skirt and prepared to make her pitch. She decided to begin with casual conversation and in the same instant, assuage her natural curiosity. "If you don't mind my asking, what's coming up at the end of the week?"

"I turn thirty-eight on Saturday," he said as he retrieved a crystal highball glass from the upper cabinet.

Six years her senior. Not too bad. Not that it mattered. "Big party planned?"

Once he filled the tumbler with ice from a bucket on the counter, then poured water into it from a pitcher he pulled from the built-in stainless refrigerator, he returned to the desk and set the glass on a coaster before her. "I hope like hell that's not going to happen. I'm not one for having people making a big deal over my birthday."

She sensed he would be that kind of man. "I have a feeling your stepmothers might be planning a big deal."

He dropped down into the chair behind the desk, leaned back and affected a relaxed posture, but his expression said he didn't exactly appreciate her conjecture. "They know better than to pull that on me."

Paris gathered he might be suffering from a severe case of the birthday blues. "Are you sure? It sounded as if at least one of them wants you to have a date for some soiree, hence the *nice girl* comment."

He sent her that sexy, crooked smile again. "If that's the case, are you volunteering to fill the role?"

If she were only that brave. Then again, if it helped

her secure the job… "I generally avoid mixing business with pleasure, although your family seemed to jump to the conclusion that my business is pleasure."

He narrowed his eyes and studied her straight on. "Speaking of that, what exactly do you do for a living?"

The suspicion in his tone ruffled her feminine feathers. "It doesn't involve a nine hundred number or a pimp, I promise you that."

Now he looked amused. "Glad you cleared the air."

So was she, and she planned to be perfectly clear. "In reality, I'm—"

"Wait. Let me guess." He inclined his head and pointed at her. "You're a stockbroker and you want to get your hands on my investments."

She might like to get her hands on something of his that happened to be a far cry from his portfolio. Since when had she become a purveyor of naughty thoughts? "Not even close."

He rubbed a palm over his chin. "I would bet the back forty you have an accounting degree."

If he only knew about her lack of accounting skills, he would never have assumed such a thing. That downfall had landed her in deep trouble and served as another reason for being there, about to beg for employment. "Believe me, math is not my forte."

"Marketing?"

In an effort to clear her parched throat, Paris took a quick sip of water. "Try again."

His gaze landed on her fingers still wrapped around the glass. "Considering your perfectly manicured nails, I'm guessing you're not a ranch hand."

"I haven't even seen a cow up close."

"Not even on your dinner plate in the form of filet mignon?"

"I'm primarily a vegetarian."

"I'm strictly a meat-and-potatoes kind of guy."

What a shocker. "I won't judge your food preferences if you won't judge mine."

"Agreed." He took off his hat to place it brim up on the desk, then forked a hand through his dark brown hair that worked well with those deadly blue eyes. "If you're a beautician, I don't need one. Just a quick round with the clippers and I'm good to go."

Yes, he was. Good enough to go anywhere he might want to take her. "No, I'm not a hairstylist. Do you give up now?"

"Yep. I'm all out of guesses."

The time had come to lay all her cards on the table, less a few secrets he didn't need to know. "I'm a commercial interior designer." Disgraced designer.

"No kidding?" he said, sounding somewhat awed over the admission.

"No kidding. And that's why I'm here. I wanted to speak to you about—"

"Hey, Dallas, I'm about to head out."

Paris shifted in her seat to see a young, buff blond guy filling the doorway. Aside from the tattered jeans and worn cowboy boots, he looked more surfer than rancher. Or body builder in light of the fit of the lime-green T-shirt hugging his muscled arms and torso.

"Where are you going now?" Dallas asked, looking and sounding none too pleased.

"To the beach for the weekend," the stranger replied as he strode to the wet bar.

Aha! Paris had pegged him right on his surfer status, though she still didn't know his relationship to the Calloways. He certainly didn't resemble Dallas.

"Did you talk to Fort yet, Worth?" Dallas asked.

"I called him," the man with the unusual name said as he pulled a soda from the fridge and popped it open. "But he's still pissed I left him high and dry and came here. He refuses to call me back."

"Figures," Dallas muttered. "By the way, does Houston know you're leaving?"

"Yeah, and Austin's agreed to hang around in case any of the heifers calve."

"That's good because Tyler's going to be gone until Monday."

Paris felt as though she'd just gone on a Cities of Texas tour. Without further hesitation, she stood to face Surfer Worth and smiled, bent on introducing herself since her potential boss evidently wasn't going to do the honors. "Hi, my name is Paris Reynolds."

Worth grinned and shook her extended hand, revealing the same dimple Dallas sported. "Pleasure to meet you, ma'am. Are you a friend of my big brother's?"

That confirmed her supposition that he was a Calloway sibling, although she couldn't recall any mention of him in any of the press releases she'd recently read. "Actually, we just met today."

Worth winked. "Well, if he doesn't treat you right, you're welcome to come to Padre Island with me. I'm a helluva lot more fun."

And way too young for her, Paris decided. Plus, she had always been attracted to brown-haired men, like the one seated not far away.

Dallas pointed at the door. "Get out, Worthless. Ms. Reynolds doesn't need you coming on to her."

Worth backed toward the exit with hands held up, palms forward. "All right. And when you find out where the hell you left your sense of humor, let me know."

With that, the younger Calloway son winked at Paris again before striding out of the room.

"I apologize for his behavior," Dallas said as he resumed holding cowboy court from his place behind the desk.

Paris dropped back down into her designated chair. "No need. He seems relatively harmless."

"He's a skirt chaser, according to his mother, and I've seen more than enough evidence of that fact."

The identity of Worth's mother didn't require a lot of guessing. "Is that Jenny?"

"Yeah, my father's third wife. Maria is the second."

"And your mother is?"

Dallas's gaze drifted away for a moment. "Gone. She died when I was pretty young."

"I'm sorry, Dallas." And she sincerely was. "I'm sure that's been really difficult for you."

"Not so much," he said. "I barely remember her. Now let's get back to the reason why you're here."

Being summarily dismissed wasn't all that surprising to Paris. Most men clammed up when it came to emotional issues, including her own father. "Well, as I was saying, I'm a commercial interior designer, and since it's apparent you'll need my services soon, I'm here to apply for the position."

He frowned. "Why do you believe I need an interior decorator?"

She wasn't certain if he was kidding, or he really didn't have a clue. "Look, I saw an article in the San Antonio paper about this Texas Extreme project and how you're going to cater to people who want to enjoy the whole high-risk rodeo experience." Though she couldn't imagine why anyone would want to do that. "I also read about your plans to build a lodge to house your guests, and that's where I come in. I would like the opportunity to oversee the design of that lodge."

"We haven't even broken ground yet," he said. "In fact, we haven't seen the final plans from the architect."

That could definitely work to her advantage. "All the better. If I'm involved in the beginning, then I can make suggestions that will only enhance the guests' experience. I have extensive knowledge in hotel design. I have a strong attention to detail and—"

"Ms. Reynolds—"

"Paris."

"Okay, Paris, first of all, these guests are wannabe cowboys. They don't need a fancy room. They only need a bunk and a bathroom. Hell, they might be satisfied with an outhouse and a creek."

The thought made her shudder. Yet he had made a good point, darn it. Still… "What if some of them want to bring their wives? Women have much higher standards. What if some of the wives or girlfriends want to participate, too?"

He mulled that over a moment before addressing her again. "I hadn't thought about that."

Now she was getting somewhere. "Have you given any consideration to the kitchen? You are having one installed, aren't you? Or will you be roasting marshmallows and wieners?"

He favored her with a sexy grin. "That's a thought."

"Seriously? A wiener roast for every meal?"

"Maybe that's not a great idea. But the kitchen doesn't have to be all that elaborate. Just the basics."

He truly didn't grasp the concept of hospitality. "How many people do you plan to house at one time?"

"Fifty if we're at capacity, but we want to be able to accommodate more in the future."

"Feeding fifty hungry men and/or women will require more than a four-burner stove, a side-by-side refrigerator and a single oven. You'll need commercial-grade appliances, plenty of prep space—"

"I understand what you're saying," he said, effectively cutting her off. "But we don't plan to open for business for a year, maybe longer if we can't get all the facilities set up by then. Not only do we have to build the lodge, we have to build a new arena and catch pens, plus a first-aid station and acquire rodeo stock. I wouldn't even need you for a good six months."

She would be destitute in two months. The unwelcome sense of extreme anxiety came home to roost, prompting Paris to make a final plea. "Again, you would be better off hiring me now than fixing something later. That will only cost you more money. I could meet with the architect before the plans are finalized. I could take care of all the details from the ground up. Besides, I live in San Antonio and since that's only an hour and a half away, that's convenient for us both. And I'm going to work cheaper than many firms you might decide to hire, but I don't do cheap work or cut corners. To be perfectly honest, you can't do better than me. And most important, I really, really need this job."

He tilted his head again and eyed her suspiciously. "If you're so good at it, why is that?"

She'd gone too far with the tirade, and probably blown any chance at the opportunity to oversee his project. Yet she was somewhat bolstered by the fact he hadn't kicked her out…yet. "Due to personal circumstances beyond my control, I've been forced to start over, but I won't bother you with the details. I would like to show you my work."

As she drew a breath, Paris fumbled for the briefcase resting on the floor and lifted it up. "I have my portfolio right here if you care to take a quick look."

Dallas sat in silence for a few moments while Paris's pulse raced out of control. "I'm sure you're more than qualified for the job," he finally said, "but like I told you, I don't see the need to hire a decorator—"

"Designer," Paris corrected without regard to helping her cause.

"Hiring a *designer* right now doesn't make much sense to me."

Plagued with the bitter taste of defeat, Paris stood. "Fine, but you should be aware, in six months, I might not be available." She might even be in jail. Or worse—

living with her folks on a potato farm in Idaho. "It's been a pleasure to meet you."

Dallas came to his feet and rounded the desk. "One question before you leave. What exactly did you mean by having to start over?"

She certainly wasn't prepared to get into that, but if it meant he might possibly reconsider, she would tell him everything. Almost everything. "Okay, as long as you understand I'm not looking for pity."

"Understood."

Oh, how she hated having to explain the sordid details. "Almost two years ago, my ex-husband left in the middle of the night, took every penny I owned and then took off to the Dominican Republic to get a quickie divorce."

The anger that flashed in his eyes took her aback. "Where is the bastard now?"

"Still there, with my hard-earned money and a new girlfriend. Shortly thereafter, the firm where I'd been working for eight years laid me off. I have very few funds to maintain my apartment for much longer, so I might be forced to move in with my family until I get back on my feet." That last part had wounded her pride beyond belief. The part she'd left out—the reasons why she'd lost her job—had caused her great shame.

He attempted a slight smile. "I can relate to living with family."

"Your stepmothers live with you?"

"No, they live in the main house. I built my own place a few years ago. But I see them every day, whether I want to or not."

They just stood there in uncomfortable silence until Paris decided to end the meeting and escape from her humiliating revelations. She retrieved a card from her bag's side pocket and offered it to him. "If you happen to change your mind, here's my contact information. If not, I wish you the best of luck with your new venture."

"Good luck to you, too," he said as he escorted her to the door. "And if I happen to need a date to a surprise birthday party, I just might give you a call."

Oh, sure he would. In some ways she wished he would. Who wouldn't want to spend an evening with a gorgeous macho guy? And since he obviously wasn't going to hire her…"You know, I just might take you up on the invitation."

Without gauging his response, Paris worked her way back to the front office and out the door, pausing only long enough to tell both mothers to have a good day. Once she slid into her car, she experienced overwhelming dejection over the epic failure. But she refused to cry. She'd already done enough of that to last a lifetime.

"Why in the hell did you let her leave, Dallas?"

At the moment, a lecture from Maria—his long time maternal influence—was the very last thing Dallas needed. He still hadn't gotten over the impact of the pretty green-eyed, golden-haired, determined woman named after a European city who had landed on his doorstep. He didn't quite understand his reaction to her, either. A strong reaction that had had him wanting to suggest things to her that any man with an ounce of honor wouldn't dare mention to a woman he'd just met. And if Maria Leone Calloway could read his mind, she would nix the speech and wash his mouth out with homemade soap even if he hadn't uttered a dirty word.

He cleared the uncomfortable hitch from his throat and shifted in his chair. "I don't know why her departure is bothering you, Mom. I figured you didn't like her all that much."

Without invitation, the current burr in his backside took the seat Paris Reynolds had vacated a few minutes before. "She's a little too uppity in my opinion, *mijo*. But as bad as I hate to admit it, Jenny was right about one thing. You need to find a woman, and maybe this Paris is that woman."

Dallas rocked back in his chair and sighed. "First of all, you both need to forget about that. It's too late. Secondly, I've come to terms with staying single and you just need to accept it."

Maria narrowed her dark eyes. "You're telling me you're going to let your no-account little brother gain control over this ranch?"

The thought left a bad taste in his mouth. "Blame your husband for putting that stupid marriage codicil in the will, although it still doesn't make any sense why Dad would leave this place to Fort. From what Jenny says, the kid was a rebel most of his life, plus he already owns the horse farm in Louisiana."

Maria tightened the band securing her braid, a nervous habit for as long as Dallas could remember. "You're right. It doesn't make a damn bit of sense what J.D. did, particularly since Fort wants nothing to do with you or any of his brothers. Then again, what your father did to me and Jenny didn't make any sense, either."

Dallas would never forget that day six years ago when during the reading of his father's will, he'd not only discovered he had twin half-brothers, he'd learned his father had been living as a bigamist. "I'm hoping Fort's disdain for the family will be enough for him to ignore the stipulation." Even if he wasn't banking on it.

"That's a big chance you'd be taking, Dallas," Maria said. "If you're wrong, he'll put a stop to your dream of turning this place into Texas Extreme. Hell, he could even toss you and your brothers off the property, take over the houses you all built and legally he could do it."

He knew that all too well. He also knew Fort would probably turn the place into a subdivision just to spite them. "I don't have a choice, Mom. I can't find a proper wife in four days, nor do I even want to attempt it."

The other mother—every bit the Southern belle—suddenly breezed into the room and stood behind Maria. "I think Paris is quite proper and sophisticated, and a man of your financial means and social status needs that in a life partner. If you make an effort to get to know her, who knows what could happen in a few days? You might find yourself falling hopelessly in love for the first time in your life, sugar. Why, I met your father on a Saturday night and we were married two weeks later."

"And look how that turned out, Jenny," Maria said. "Don't give him reason not to give this a shot."

Over the past few years, Dallas had learned one important thing about Jenny Parks Calloway—she was a flighty romantic who spent most of her days with stars in her eyes. "That's good in theory, Jen, but the chances of it happening are slim to none. And even if I wanted to pursue a relationship with Paris Reynolds, who's to say she would agree? And even if she did agree to go out with me, do you really think she'd jump at the chance to marry me two days later? Get real."

"She sounded pretty desperate to us," Jenny chimed in, then clamped her mouth closed after Maria shot her a nasty look over her shoulder.

Dallas wasn't all that shocked, but he was pretty pissed off over the intrusion. "You two were listening to our conversation?"

"Just a little bit," Jenny said sheepishly. "Your phone's intercom was on."

He looked at the key pad, noted the button was depressed and then muttered a few mild oaths. "Why didn't you tell me?"

"We didn't want to disturb you, *mijo*," Maria said.

Dallas didn't buy that for a minute. "You wanted to eavesdrop. Regardless of how desperate Paris might be, I don't see her as the kind of woman who'd agree to marry a stranger in exchange for a job. And I'm not the kind of man who would ask that of any woman."

Jenny put on her sweeter-than-honey expression. "Sugar, I love my son, but I also know Fort doesn't deserve this place given how much grief he's showered on me and Worth. Why don't you just invite Paris to dinner tonight and see what happens?"

He'd like to see what happened, but not in the way she was thinking. "I'm sure she's already halfway to

San Antonio by now and I've got a lot do before I fly to Houston in two days."

"You can take one night off," Maria stated, a totally out-of-character comment.

"Yes, you can, for the cause," Jenny added. "Now go after her, sugar, and escort her back here. I can make you both my famous chateaubriand."

He saw one big problem with that, and a prime excuse to halt all the nonsense. "She's a vegetarian."

Maria shook her head. "Yeah, we heard her say that, but it's not normal. Not normal at all."

"We'll work around it," Jenny said. "I'll make a wonderful assortment of spring vegetables. That will allow Dallas and Paris to get to know each other better in an intimate setting, not a crowded restaurant."

Dallas barked out a laugh. "Sure, while the two of you hang out in the next room, listening to every word we say."

Jenny raised her hand like she was about to take an oath. "I swear I will leave as soon as the food is served. Maria will, too. Right?"

Maria stared up at Jenny. "Why do you need me there anyway?"

"For moral support," Jenny answered. "And you can make Dallas his usual T-bone, since that's not my forte."

Maria sighed. "It's easy. Remove the horns, slap it on the stove, make sure it's not mooing and put it on the plate."

Jenny ignored Maria and took his hand. "Sugar, we'll work out the dinner details. In the meantime, you just have to convince Paris to join you by telling her you want to discuss the particulars of the job, sort of like an interview. Then you can see what comes up after that."

He had a sneaking suspicion he knew exactly what would come up if he didn't get a rein on his libido. Logical or not, he did like the plan, if for no other reason than to spend a little more time with Paris. As far as the mothers' harebrained matrimony scheme was concerned, no way would that happen.

After pushing away from the desk, he stood and propped his hat on his head. "All right, you two. Get to cooking and I'll go get the girl."

Two

Seated in her compact sedan, Paris stared at the private number displayed on her phone. Normally she would ignore the call, but some mysterious force propelled her to answer. "Hello?"

"Where are you right now?"

Overcome with sudden paranoia, she looked around the almost empty lot for some seedy no-account who'd magically come upon her cell number. "Who is this?"

"Sorry. It's Dallas Calloway. Are you back in San Antonio?"

"No," she said after she'd regained enough composure to speak. "I'm at a convenience store somewhere between Cotulla and Dilley. Or maybe I've already passed Dilley and missed it when I blinked."

"Right off the interstate?"

"Yes. It's a red-and-white building with some weird creature on the sign, but I can't see the name from here."

"I know the place. Stay put. I'll be there in a few."

Paris didn't have the opportunity to say another word before the line went dead, leaving her with a laundry list of questions bombarding her brain. Why would he want to come after her? Had she left something important at the office? She glanced at the passenger seat to verify the presence of her briefcase, although only a few moments ago she'd just carried it into the store to pay for gas and buy a snack. Speaking of snacks…she yanked down the visor and pulled up the vanity mirror to check for the presence of chocolate, which she found smeared in the corner of her mouth.

Paris scrambled around in the center console for a napkin, then swiped furiously over the offensive spot while cursing herself for being such a cliché. Have stress, grab candy. Preferably chocolate candy. Dark, light, didn't matter. As long as it contained cocoa and no nuts.

After reapplying her lipstick, and tightening the hair band securing the low twist at her nape, she waited for the enigmatic cowboy to arrive in a pickup, or possibly ride up on his trusty horse.

The first assumption had been correct, she realized, when a large dual-wheeled black monstrosity of a truck pulled in the space to her right and its dashing driver left the cab.

As Dallas approached the door, Paris powered down her window to find out what his surprise appearance was all about. "Did I forget something?" she asked as soon as he arrived.

"Nope," he said. "But I forgot to ask you something."

"What would that be, pray tell?"

"If you'd care to stay for dinner."

Only moments ago, she'd consumed a large bar of candy and washed it down with cola so dinner wasn't all that appealing. But maybe this was his way of saying he might be considering her for the position after all. "Dinner would be nice, but wouldn't it have been much easier for you to call me and ask me to come back rather than you drive all the way here?"

"Yep, that fifteen-minute drive was a real hardship, but here the West is still wild, and the men go after their women."

She'd give him a speech on the death of chauvinism if he didn't look so gorgeous displaying that grin and a delightful dimple. "Far be it from me to question archaic tradition."

He leaned over and folded his arms on the window's ledge. "Are you going to follow me home, or do you want to ride with me and I'll bring you back later to get your car?"

Although he seemed harmless enough, Paris wasn't stupid. If she didn't have her vehicle, she couldn't determine when it was time to go. "I know the way now. I'll drive."

He pushed away from the car and straightened. "Fine by me. See you in a bit."

In less time than it took Paris to fasten her seat belt, Dallas shot out of the lot on spinning tires, kicking up a flurry of dust in his wake as he turned onto the access road. She took a little more time following suit, still questioning the reason behind his surprise invitation.

Yet life wasn't without risk, and she'd taken plenty in her formative years. Some had turned out well, others, not so much. She hoped this risk proved to be a good one.

After traveling ten or so miles, she found Dallas had pulled over on the shoulder to wait for her. He seemed to slow down to accommodate her caution, and remained that way until they turned off the interstate and onto the rural road leading to the ranch.

Once they traveled through the elaborate stone entry containing the iron sign announcing their arrival at the D Bar C, Dallas drove past the office where the barren terrain took a dramatic turn. Paris glanced from the road long enough to ogle the massive white rock ranch house to her left as Dallas continued on. They passed by several other large houses set back off the road, each one appearing to include transplanted trees, lovely landscaping, first-rate barns and expensive vehicles, including one black Porsche that she would wager belonged to Worth. After Dallas took a left, pavement soon turned to gravel as they navigated through pastureland lined with barbwire fence and dotted with mesquite.

They soon passed a large pond lined with weeping willows where a two-story, expansive home came into view, dealing Paris another stunning mental blow. The structure was also stone trimmed with cedar accents, like the rest of the residences, only this one had a gleaming silver metal roof and seemed to be twice the size, as well as a tad more elaborate. If she didn't know better, she would have thought she'd happened upon a resort hotel.

Dallas pulled beneath the portico and Paris followed his lead, half expecting to be greeted by a parking attendant. When that didn't happen, she slid out of the car and joined her host for the evening at the entry. "Nice place you have here," she said as he opened one of the heavy pine double doors.

"It'll do," he replied with surprising nonchalance.

It would more than do, she realized after she stepped over the threshold. A grand staircase with a wrought iron banister centered in the soaring foyer, and dark slate floors could be deemed somewhat elegant. Yet that was where the elegance ended, right before the West began.

As Paris trailed behind Dallas into the great room, the cowboy culture came shining through in the floor-to-ceiling rock fireplace anchoring the room along with the macho leather furniture in shades of gray and black. And hanging from the towering ceiling, a chandelier, for lack of a better term, appeared to be made out of metallic animal horns, although she would swear they weren't authentic. At least she hoped not.

"Welcome to Dallas's little piece of heaven, Paris," Jenny said as she floated into the room wearing a frilly pink apron and a vibrant smile.

Odd that Dallas didn't have household staff and had to rely on his stepmother to play hostess. "Thanks for having me, and I have to agree. This place is paradise."

Jenny's grin deepened. "You should see the veranda overlooking the pool, which is where you two will dine so you can watch the sunset. The view is breathtaking."

Dallas frowned. "I'm thinking the dining room might be better since it's still fairly hot outside and the mosquitoes are big as airplanes."

Jenny waved her hand in a dismissive gesture. "Oh, posh, Dallas. You don't have a romantic bone in your body. Besides, the temperature will go down with the sun and it's too early in the year for a lot of bugs, including mosquitoes."

A sunset dinner was conducive to romance, but Paris was not in the market for wining and dining or mosquitoes. "The dining room will be fine." When Jenny looked absolutely disappointed, she added, "Or the veranda. I'm sure the sunset is very impressive."

"The veranda it is," Jenny said as she started to back away. "Dinner will be ready very soon and I assure you, Paris, I'm preparing a delectable vegetarian meal. In the meantime, Dallas can give you the VIP tour. His master suite is to die for."

She questioned the wisdom in viewing Dallas's bedroom. "I'm looking forward to it. The tour, I mean."

Jenny smiled before she hurried away, leaving Dallas and Paris standing in the middle of the great room cloaked in uncomfortable silence.

"Are you ready for the tour?" he asked.

As long as he didn't get too close to her in the boudoir; otherwise she might forget herself in the shadow of that smile. "I'm more than a little curious, so lead the way."

"Okay. Follow me."

And she did, up the stairs, trying desperately to avoid studying his butt before they took an immediate right at the top landing. They walked by several closed doors before reaching the end of the corridor where Dallas paused at a pair of double doors.

"Prepare yourself," he said. "You're about to see where all the action happens."

Holding her breath, Paris expected to discover a large bed, but she only saw what appeared to be a cowboy man cave with an at least seventy-inch television screen, a large old-fashioned bar straight out of a saloon and a series of round wooden tables and straight-backed chairs. She strolled toward a large glass display case to her right that housed trophies and belt buckles and trinkets from days past. "Is this the Dallas Calloway Hall of Fame?"

"Not exactly," he said from behind her. "If I had my way, those things would've stayed in the trunk in the tack room."

She glanced at him over one shoulder. "You should be proud of these. Not many men can lay claim to being a three-time world champion all-around cowboy."

"Funny, that's what Maria said." He came to her side, showing his handsome profile to full advantage. "She set this up after I built the house."

Time to get to know him a bit better. "You two are close, huh?"

He streaked a palm over his neck. "Yeah. She's the only mother I've ever really known. Then Jen came into the mix and now I have two mothers. Double trouble. They mean well but sometimes they're both a little too motherly."

"Right down to choosing your mate?"

He shot her a smile, throwing her for a mental loop.

"They try but I don't listen to them when it comes to my choice in female companionship."

That led Paris to a question she'd been dying to ask, perhaps at her own detriment if she dared. "You really don't have a girlfriend waiting somewhere in the wings?"

He turned those silver-blue eyes on her. "Nope. I've had a couple of steady girlfriends in the past, but rodeo and relationships didn't mix well."

"Apparently you no longer rodeo, so do you see yourself eventually settling down?"

He sent her an odd look before he brought his attention back to the mementos from his past. "Only if and when the time is right."

"I'm sure you're considered quite the catch in these parts. Probably throughout the state."

He turned and leaned a shoulder against the case. "I've had my share of propositions, but it's kind of hard to tell if they're more interested in my personality, or my personal finances."

Or his stellar physical attributes. "I'm sure more than a few are drawn to the cowboy fantasy and the notion you'll scoop them up and ride off into the sunset."

"Is that your fantasy?"

Not until that moment. Not until he favored her with that winning, dimpled grin again. "My exposure to cowboys has been nonexistent, so I'd have to say no."

He inched a little closer. "Now that you've been exposed, do you think you might change your mind?"

Heaven help her, he was flirting like a teenage jock. And she responded like an adolescent schoolgirl with a self-conscious smile. "The jury is still out. I'll let you know after dinner."

"And I'll do my best to show you there's something to be said for the cowboy way."

They stood there in silence, tension as thick as a morning haze hanging over them as Dallas's focus landed on her mouth. Paris sensed if she moved just a little closer, gave him just a little encouragement, he might actually kiss her. And she might actually hurl caution to the warm wind and let him.

The sound of staccato footsteps interrupted the moment and drew Paris back into reality and her attention to the doorway where Jenny now stood sporting a knowing look. "Dinner is served, y'all. Just come on out to the veranda when you're finished doing whatever it is you're doing."

As soon as Jenny disappeared, Paris turned back to Dallas. "Shall we go? I'm suddenly starving."

"So am I," he replied, keeping his gaze centered on hers. "Food sounds pretty good, too."

Paris released a nervous laugh. "I can tell you have a little bad boy in you."

"Yeah, darlin', I do. But don't ever doubt I'm every bit a man."

That wasn't up for debate. Paris had a sneaking suspicion if she hung around too long after dinner and let down her guard, she could very well see exactly how manly he could be.

She was getting under his skin, a dangerous prospect. He didn't need to lose all control around her, but he almost had. He didn't need a woman complicating his life, even if he couldn't deny he needed a woman. But not just any woman. *This* woman.

Dallas pushed his empty plate aside and watched as Paris sipped at the second mint julep Jenny had served her. He'd settled for a beer, but only one, in order to keep his wits about him. He didn't know enough about Paris to bring out the usual moves, even if those fantastic green eyes had reeled him in like a trout on a fly from the minute she'd walked into the office. He brought his attention to her hands, imagined those slender fingers raking across his chest, then traveling lower to the nagging place down south that craved some female attention.

Shaking off the images, Dallas thought it best to talk, not fantasize about her being naked beneath him. "How long have you been a vegetarian?"

She dabbed at her lips then set the napkin aside. "When I started college, I was determined not to gain the typical freshman fifteen. And honestly, when I was in my teens, I was somewhat...chunky."

He couldn't even imagine that. "Are you kidding?"

"It's true. I wasn't obese, but I was anything but thin. My family moved around a lot and I tended to use food to compensate for the fact I didn't have time to make friends. Before I knew it, I was a regular porker who lived on cheeseburgers and fries."

"The only way I'd believe that is to see some pictures."

She shook her head. "No way. Besides, I think I probably destroyed all evidence."

He downed the last of the beer and pushed the mug away. "You said you moved a lot. Why is that?"

"I was a navy brat. We were rarely in one place for any length of time."

"Do you have any siblings?"

"An older sister. She's living around the corner from my parents in Idaho with her husband and three kids. My folks are so proud."

"They're not proud of you?"

She rimmed a fingertip around the edge of the glass. "Let's just say they don't understand my creative nature. Or at least my father never did. He preferred I become a nurse or teacher."

"A traditionalist, huh?"

"More like a taskmaster. It was always his way or the highway."

He could relate to that. His father was still controlling his life from the grave. "My dad never liked me devoting all my time to the rodeo. That made him a damn hypocrite since he met my mother on the circuit."

"Really?"

"Yeah. She was a barrel racer and he was a bulldogger."

"Bulldogger?"

"Steer wrestler."

She frowned. "Why would you want to wrestle a steer? That sounds rather dangerous."

He chuckled over her lack of comprehension. "Sorry. I'm just surrounded by women who lived with rodeo cowboys. Most of the time they think they know more about it than I do."

After downing the last of her drink, she took off her jacket and laid it in her lap, revealing a sleeveless silk top that sparked his imagination. And suddenly he started to sweat.

"Well, you'll never have to worry about that with me," she began, "because obviously I know nothing about the rodeo. Not that I'm averse to learning. I'm a quick study."

Just seeing her bare arms, and a hint of cleavage, brought to mind a few lessons involving his second favorite sport. "I'm a good teacher."

Smiling, she bent her elbow on the table and supported her cheek with her palm. "When is my first lesson?"

He wanted to suggest tonight, but the fact her voice sounded a little thick led him to believe she might be feeling the effects of the alcohol. "You name the place and the time, and I'll be there."

After a moment's hesitation, she straightened and stared out at the horizon. "This place really surprised me. I was expecting a lot more desertlike terrain, not all this green pastureland. The scenery is really beautiful."

So was she, and the fact she didn't seem to realize that only elevated Dallas's opinion of her. "Yeah, when the sky turns orange at sunset, it makes all the mesquite trees look good."

She sent him a smile. "Where are you going to put the lodge?"

"On the east side of the property. We've surveyed about five acres that will be dedicated to Texas Extreme."

"How many acres do you have?"

"Ten thousand."

Her eyes went wide. "Wow. That's a lot of land."

He resisted reaching across the table and pushing the strand of hair away from her cheek. "We have a large herd of cattle. In fact, Texas Extreme is going to offer the experience of a good old-fashioned cattle drive, including a camp-out under the stars, complete with a chuck wagon."

"That actually sounds fun. I'd like to join you."

"You'd have to learn to ride a horse first."

"I'm game, as long as it's a gentle horse."

"That can be arranged. I have a good gelding. He's so broke I'd put a five-year-old on him."

"That would be about my speed."

"Something tells me you'd be a natural."

Her cheeks turned a light shade of pink. "Thanks, but don't count on it. I'm not sure I've ever been a natural at anything except designing."

That put all sorts of questionable images in his mind. "I doubt that. In fact, I'm fairly sure you're a natural at several things."

She barked out a soft laugh. "I can't think of one."

"I can, but I'm guessing your ex never tapped into your innate abilities."

"My ex rarely tapped into anything after our first year of marriage."

Without giving it a thought, Dallas reached over and pushed that sliver of golden hair away from her face. "The man had to be an idiot. Is that why you divorced him?"

She suddenly looked more than a little uncomfortable. "He divorced me, remember? Not that I thought the marriage had any chance of surviving at that juncture. Anyway, I should probably be going before it gets any later."

He really didn't want her to leave but he had no one to blame but himself for bringing up past history. "It's barely eight."

"And I still have to drive back to San Antonio."

When Paris pushed back from the table, came to her feet and swayed, Dallas stood and caught her arm. "Are you okay?"

She pinched the bridge of her nose with her fingers. "I was fine until I got up. Guess I'm a little tired. That drink went straight to my head."

As he'd predicted, Jenny's mint juleps had claimed another unsuspecting victim. He should've warned Paris that she could be heavy-handed with the bourbon. "Come to think of it, you had two."

She sent him a shaky smile. "I did, didn't I?"

"Yeah, you did, which means you're in no shape to drive."

Her stern expression didn't take away from her fantastic face. "I can't very well stay here."

"You can, and you will. I have several guest rooms. Five, in fact. Take your pick." If he had his way, she'd pick his room. But he'd been taught never to take advantage of a woman under the influence.

"I didn't pack a bag," she protested. "I'm sure if I lie down for a little while, I'll be fine."

He didn't have much faith in that. "We'll see how

you feel later, but I'm not going to let you get behind the wheel tonight if I think you're not fit to drive. End of discussion."

Clasping her elbow, Dallas led Paris through the double sliding doors, into the sunroom and guided her to the great room. He took one look at the towering staircase and decided showing her to his downstairs quarters would be the better part of valor.

He continued down the corridor and past the kitchen where he noticed Jenny cleaning up the dishes. He didn't dare stop although he knew he'd have to do some serious explaining if she caught sight of them heading to the bedroom. He'd wager his inheritance she had. Not a problem. He had a bone to pick with her over the booze.

Once they arrived at the back of the house, he let go of Paris long enough to open the double doors before grasping her arm to steady her.

She took him by surprise when she wrenched out of his hold and headed to the bed. "This looks heavenly," she said as she fell back on the mattress and laughed. "What a lovely guest room."

"It's my room," he muttered. "I wasn't sure you could make it up the stairs."

She giggled again when she kicked off her shoes and one landed on top of the dresser several feet away, barely missing the mirror. "Are you trying to ruin my reputation, sir?"

"I'm trying to keep you from breaking your neck." He crossed the room and held out his hands. "Hop up so I can turn down the covers."

She accepted the gesture but instead of stepping

aside, she stepped right into his arms. And then she did the one thing he'd been avoiding all night, yet wanted more than anything. She planted her mouth on his.

She looked like a saint and kissed like a sinner. Oh, yeah, she was a natural. She had mighty fine lips and met his tongue stroke for stroke. He roved his palms down her slender back and paused right before he reached her butt, which took a lot of effort.

He intended to stop it before they went too far. Stop short before it went too deep. But when she pressed that sweet body against his, he tossed all those well-intentioned plans to the plains. And the longer this went on, the more he wanted to take her back onto the bed… or ignore all formality and take her down to the floor.

Without warning, Paris pulled away and touched her fingertips to her mouth like she'd been burned. "I'm not normally that bold."

He liked her *that* bold. "You're not thinking straight."

"I'm a little bit tipsy," she said, her speech slurred. "I came here to convince you to hire me, not to drink and make out with you."

That made him feel like an oversexed teenager. "It was just a kiss, Paris." One knock-em-dead kiss. "And I'm the one who should've stopped it."

Paris dropped down on the edge of the mattress. "I'm really not…normally…like this." She followed the comment with a hiccup and a giggle.

"You've got a good excuse," he said as he pulled her up again and set her aside to turn down the comforter. "Now lie down and sleep it off."

"Okay," she said through a yawn. "But don't let me

sleep too long. I have to…" Her eyes drifted closed then opened again. "Hmmm. I have to do something tomorrow but I can't remember what."

Dallas suspected she'd be there all night, and he'd be spending the evening in another bed, wishing he was beside her. He hooked a thumb behind him. "The bathroom's there if you need it. Make yourself at home."

She pulled the band that secured her low ponytail and set it on the nightstand before she perched on the edge of the mattress. "Thank you, Dallas Calloway. You're a nice man, and I'm sorry I'm not acting like a nice girl."

He liked his girls a little naughty, he started to say, but began backing to the door when he noticed how sexy she looked with that blond hair curling around her shoulders. "No need to apologize. Just get some rest."

She stretched her arms over her head and sent him a sleepy smile. "Since I probably blew my chances at the job, I wouldn't mind another kiss good-night." She tapped her cheek and smiled. "Just a peck."

He might laugh at that if he hadn't been so damn uncomfortable, or tempted to do more than give her *just* a peck. "We'll talk later when you're sober. I'll check on you in a bit."

Before he traded in his honor and gave in to animal urges, Dallas rushed out of the room, closed the door behind him and then headed down the hall to confront the culprit who'd created the chaos. Once he reached the kitchen, he found Jenny loading the last of the dishes into the washer. "What in the hell did you put in those drinks?"

Jenny turned toward him and had the gall to look

surprised. "Why, honey, just the usual. A little mint, some sugar and water, bourbon. And maybe a touch of tequila."

That explained a lot. "You added tequila on top of the bourbon?"

She didn't bother to look contrite. "Yes. It gives the julep that special kick everyone raves about."

"It kicked my date right into drunk mode."

Jenny grinned. "Your date?"

"Guest," he corrected, although he didn't see much point in getting the details right.

"Maybe I put a little too much alcohol into the drink," she said, "but I thought it would help Paris relax."

"Hell, she's relaxed all right. She's passed out in my bed."

"Then why are you in here?"

He was asking himself that same question. "Because there is no way I'm going to seduce a woman who's intoxicated."

Jenny leaned back against the counter. "Of course you wouldn't, sugar. You're too good for that. However, she won't be drunk in the morning."

Of all the confounded suggestions. "I'm going to check on Paris and then I'm going upstairs."

"I'll have a nice breakfast waiting for the two of you in the morning."

"Great."

Without further comment, Dallas turned around and nearly ran into his other stepmother. "'Night," he muttered, looking for a quick escape.

Maria had other ideas, he realized, when she grabbed his arm. "Why is the woman still here?"

He didn't have the energy to explain. "Ask Jenny," he said as he brushed past her and headed toward his bedroom.

Once there, he opened the door to find Paris curled up on her side, the covers shoved to the end of the bed. She'd stripped down to a white strapless bra and damn if she hadn't taken off her skirt, giving him a prime view of a pair of lacy, black panties.

Damn, damn, damn...

He should probably turn tail and run, but he worried about leaving her all night in her current state. He could crawl in next to her, or he could be the man Maria had raised him to be. A gentleman.

With that in mind, he strode into the bathroom, dressed in his boxers and a T-shirt, then prepared to sleep in the lounger. But before he settled in for the duration, he paused a few moments to study the gorgeous woman in his bed.

With her arm crooked beneath her head, her hair a sexy, tangled mess, she looked somewhat innocent in sleep, and someone he wouldn't mind waking up to in the morning. He liked her wit, her brain and her body. Definitely her body. Too bad he hadn't met her a year ago, when he still had time to court a woman in an effort to meet his match, and circumvent the terms of the will.

But unfortunately that time had passed, and unless he wanted to propose to someone he'd met only a few hours ago, he could just let go of that pipe dream. Then something suddenly occurred to him. Something the mothers had suggested.

Nah. That would be too weird, not to mention she would never agree to it.

Following a quick shower, Dallas took one last look at the pretty lady, turned off the lights and kicked back in the lounge chair. He still had trouble shutting down his thoughts for several reasons, including the damned deadline on the will. He'd be better served if he accepted his fate—his youngest brother would have controlling interest over the ranch. Short of a miracle, that would come to pass. Unless...

Maybe the harebrained idea could work if he handled it right. If he made it worth Paris's while. Or she could laugh in his face and leave. Still, it couldn't hurt to ask, if he found the courage to do it. Hell, he'd ridden some of the rankest bulls in the world. He could propose a marriage pact to a woman.

Probably best to sleep on it for now and decide in the morning—if he actually got any sleep at all.

Three

Shaking off the fog of sleep, Paris came into consciousness slowly in reaction to a ribbon of light landing on her face. She opened her eyes and squinted at first, until she spotted the man with an open chambray shirt sitting in the chair in the corner, putting on his boots. Her eyes went wide when she remembered her current location—a stranger's bed.

Then it all came back to her, one frame at a time, like a mortifying slide show. Dinner with Dallas Calloway. Two drinks. Getting drunk. Getting into his bed. And that kiss she'd instigated.

Paris resisted the urge to pull the covers over her head and hide away until he left. Or she could choose the mature path and apologize again for her stupid behavior.

After scooting up against the tufted leather headboard, Paris pushed her hair away from her face and cleared her throat to garner his attention. "What time is it?"

He glanced at her, rose to his feet and began buttoning his shirt, but not before she caught a good glimpse of his toned chest, ridged abdomen and the thin happy trail leading to his open fly. "It's after nine," he said. "I thought for a minute there you might sleep until lunchtime."

She thought for a minute there she might swallow her tongue due to his sheer male perfection. "You should have woken me sooner."

"I tried."

"Apparently not very hard."

"I nearly shook your shoulder off, but you didn't budge." He cracked a crooked smile. "How's your head?"

"Fuzzy." But not so fuzzy that she couldn't recall what a fool she'd made of herself.

"Need an aspirin?" he asked as he tucked his shirt into the jeans' waistband.

She needed an escape route when she noticed her skirt and top hanging on the end of the bedpost. "No, I'm fine," she said as she clutched the covers tighter. "I do need to get dressed and go home."

He barked out a laugh. "That's usually my morning line."

It suddenly occurred to her she might not remember everything about their evening, although she couldn't imagine forgetting *that*. "Uh, we didn't do anything... you know."

He buckled his belt and approached the side of the bed. "Unfortunately 'you know' wasn't involved. You did strip down to your underwear, but I didn't look."

"I've definitely heard that before." She determined an amendment would be best before he assumed she slept around. "From my ex-husband, and he was telling the truth. He rarely looked at me the last few years of our wedded non-bliss."

"Your husband sounds like an idiot. No offense."

"No offense taken. You've pegged him right, although my actions last evening would probably qualify as idiotic. I'm so sorry I subjected you to that."

He grabbed an off-white straw cowboy hat hanging from a hook near the door. "Look, you had a little too much to drink. It happens."

"Not to me," she muttered. "I can't recall ever drinking so much that I took off my clothes and climbed into a stranger's bed."

"Darlin', since all you did was climb into my bed, I think you can stop worrying about your actions."

"But I kissed you. Or at least I think I did."

His grin expanded. "Oh, yeah, you did. And you won't hear me complainin' about that at all."

At least that was reassuring. "I want to be clear I have never done anything like this before."

"Kissed someone?"

"Kissed someone I just met."

"I kind of like knowing I was your first."

"I like knowing you're not completely disgusted with me."

"Nothing about you disgusts me, sweetheart." He

settled the hat on his head and smiled. "Stay in bed as long as you'd like, and I'll see you in a bit."

"In bed?" Now why had she said something so leading and ludicrous?

He didn't seem at all affected by the faux pas. "Is that an invitation?"

She shook her aching head. "No. Just proof that I sometimes speak before I think."

He winked. "That's too bad."

Paris fought the temptation to tell him she'd reconsidered. "Where are you going now?"

"I have to check on some of the livestock."

"Well, I guess I'll just say goodbye then. I'll probably be on my way home before you get back."

"You can't leave yet. Jenny went to town this morning and bought you a dress and some underclothes and laundered them. She left them in the bathroom along with some toiletries. She's also keeping breakfast warm for you."

Jenny could be nominated for Southern sainthood, in her opinion. But how embarrassing to have one of the Calloway stepmothers learn she'd spent the night in the stepson's bed. "Although I appreciate the gesture, that's not really necessary. I'll just put on the clothes I wore last night and get out of your hair."

"I want you to stay a while longer so we can talk."

"About what?"

"Business," he said as he clasped the knob and opened the door. "So don't go anywhere."

Paris fought the urge to salute over his demanding tone, but Dallas had already disappeared before she could deliver the gesture. Assured he had left the premises, she slipped out of bed and wandered into the bathroom. Spa bathroom.

The beige marble tub seemed as large as her whole apartment, and so was the stone shower. She had a good mind to take a soak, but she didn't want to prolong her stay in Dallas's domain or delay the breakfast Jenny had prepared.

She retrieved shampoo and shower gel from the basket on the double vanity, gathered a towel from the heated rack on the wall, then took a quick spray until she finally felt somewhat refreshed and energized.

She dressed in the aforementioned underwear, and donned the yellow sundress hanging on a hook on the back of the door. Evidently Jenny had thought of everything, right down to the matching sandals and hair dryer.

After completing the morning ritual, Paris strode back into the bedroom where she thankfully found her case that held her makeup bag. She didn't have her complete beauty arsenal, but she did have mascara and lip gloss, which would have to do.

After pulling her hair back into a low ponytail, Paris carefully folded her suit, shoved it into the bag and then headed toward the luscious scents wafting through the hallway. Once there, she found Jenny standing at the massive six-burner stainless stove, flipping pancakes, surrounded by a chef's dream kitchen. She had finally uncovered the one place that shouted ultramodern, not macho rustic.

"Good morning, Jenny," she said as she sent her a somewhat self-conscious smile.

The friendly stepmom favored her with a bright grin. "Good morning to you, sugar. Did you sleep well?"

"Like a rock." Like a drunken sailor. "The mint juleps saw to that."

Jenny pushed the spatula under one cake and slid it onto a plate. "I am so sorry, sugar. I didn't know you were such a lightweight."

Paris leaned against the cabinet adjacent to the huge fridge and rested an elbow on the gray quartz countertop. "I really don't drink too often. Just the occasional glass of wine."

Jenny sent her a sideways glance. "Would you like a mimosa? Or perhaps a screwdriver. Nothing relieves a hangover better than that old hair of the hound dog."

The thought twisted her stomach into a knot. "Heavens no. I mean, no thank you. I wouldn't mind some orange juice, without the champagne or vodka."

Jenny retrieved a pitcher of juice from the refrigerator, poured Paris a glass and handed it to her. "You're not from the South, are you, sugar?"

"No. Why?"

"Because good Southern girls like their toddies now and again."

Now and again could possibly be an understatement when it came to Jenny. "I'm not really from anywhere. My family traveled all over the country during my youth."

That earned Paris a sympathetic look. "Everyone

should have a place to call home, honey. Mine was the New Orleans area, until I moved here."

Paris had fond memories of New Orleans, the place where she'd headed her first hotel design project. Little had she known that a few years later, she would suffer a major fall from grace. "Do you miss Louisiana?"

Jenny shrugged. "At times, but I can always go back whenever I choose."

She gestured toward a small bistro table set near a bank of windows at the end of the expansive kitchen. "Have a seat, sugar. How many slices of bacon with your pancakes?"

Apparently Jenny had forgotten the meal she'd prepared the night before. "None, please. And only one pancake."

The woman looked as if Paris had uttered the ultimate blasphemy. "Oh, that's right. You're a vegetarian."

After setting her glass on the round table, Paris pulled back a cute red chair and sat. The color definitely indicated a woman's touch, and most likely an unwelcome concession on Dallas's part. "I do eat eggs and some seafood. I just avoid pork, poultry and beef."

Jenny slid a plate piled high with the cakes onto the table in front of Paris. "You'd have a hard time living here, honey. Beef is a mainstay with almost every meal."

She wrinkled her nose. "Sounds like a cholesterol catastrophe to me."

After claiming the chair across from her, Jenny smiled. "You'd be surprised how good old hard work keeps that in check. I tell you, Dallas is in prime shape and in perfect health."

From what she'd seen, Paris wouldn't debate the *prime shape* part. She grabbed the pitcher of warm syrup and poured only a small amount, ignoring the pats of butter to her right. "Is Dallas not joining us for breakfast?"

Jenny laid a hand on her throat. "Oh, sugar, he gets up with the chickens. He ate at five a.m."

Paris couldn't imagine dragging out of bed at that hour, much less eating a full breakfast. "What exactly does he do at that time of the morning?"

"He tends to the ranch," came from behind Paris. "He's a rancher and that's what they do."

She didn't have to turn around to recognize the voice, but she did glance over her shoulder to see Maria Calloway pouring a cup of coffee from the carafe on the counter. "I guess that makes sense," Paris said. "I'm surprised it requires working sunup to sundown."

Maria took the chair next to Jenny and leveled her stare on Paris. "Have you ever lived on a large parcel of land?"

Paris swallowed the bite she'd just taken and rested her fork on the plate. "No, I've never lived on a farm or a ranch."

"She's never really had a home, Maria," Jenny said sympathetically. "Isn't that just so sad?"

Maria appeared unaffected by the revelation. "Then you're not accustomed to working with your hands?"

She didn't understand the reasons behind the obvious interrogation. After all, she'd be leaving in hopefully less than an hour. Then again, Dallas had mentioned a business talk, so she could be coming back to the ranch, if luck prevailed. "Any work I do with my hands involves sketching designs and using a computer keyboard."

Maria took a long drink of coffee before speaking again. "It's a hard life on a ranch. Not for the weak of spirit or faint of heart."

"It's not that bad, Maria," Jenny said. "I've adjusted just fine, but then I did spend several years on a horse farm."

Maria turned her frown on the other mother. "You spent those years throwing garden parties, so your opinion doesn't count. And since you've been here, I don't recall you even picking up a garden rake, much less muck a stall."

"Don't listen to her, Paris," Jenny said. "I planted the roses in the hedges."

"Bully for you," Maria muttered.

Feeling the need to play peacemaker, Paris decided to change the subject. "Where exactly is Dallas now?"

"In the barn, of course," Maria said. "He told me to send you there as soon as you're done eating."

Wearing a pair of sandals in a barn didn't seem wise, but anything beat dueling stepmoms. After consuming only half her food, Paris dabbed at her mouth, put the napkin aside, pushed away from the table and stood. "Ladies, it's been a pleasure meeting both of you, and thanks so much for your hospitality. Now if you'll direct me to the barn, I'll be on my way."

Maria pointed behind her. "It's that way. Big building with a big door. Can't miss it."

Jenny rose and took Paris's hand. "Sugar, I am so glad you showed up here. I know Dallas is, too."

Paris only wished she could be sure of that. "Thanks, Jenny, and if we don't see each other again, I'll always remember our meeting fondly."

"Oh, you'll be seeing her again," Maria said from her perch at the table. "Me, too. A lot."

She wanted to jump for joy. "Then he's decided to hire me?"

Jenny and Maria exchanged a strange look before Jenny regarded her again. "You could say that in a manner of speaking. Now run along, sugar. Dallas doesn't like to be kept waiting."

If a chance existed that Dallas Calloway would soon be her boss, she would run all the way to the barn.

When he noticed Paris picking her way carefully down the rock path, Dallas propped the shovel against the rough-hewn wall and smiled. His amusement was short-lived when he realized what he was about to do, and what was at stake—his future as the head of the D Bar C Ranch and his project, Texas Extreme.

If he went through with his plan, some might consider him pretty mercenary. Or insane. Or both. But at the moment, he only cared about the opinion of the good-looking woman entering the barn.

"Maria said you wanted to see me," Paris said as she balanced on one foot and shook the sawdust out of her sandal.

"Yeah," he told her, although he was seeing a little more than he should, namely a nice glimpse of the curve of her breast when she leaned over and removed the other shoe.

After she straightened and tugged at the hem on the sundress, her attention turned to some focal point behind him. "What a beautiful horse."

Dallas glanced over his shoulder to find the black gelding poking his head through the opening in the stall. "That's Raven. Even though he lost his stud status years ago, he still knows a beautiful woman when he sees one."

A slight blush colored her cheeks. "He must not get out much."

Dallas still couldn't get why she didn't realize her worth. He'd be happy to take a turn at trying to convince her. But not now. Not yet. He had something more pressing that required her consideration. "How was breakfast?"

She leaned back against the opposite wall. "Wonderful. Maria said you wanted to speak with me."

"Yeah. I thought I could show you around."

"Around where?"

"The barn." *Although the bedroom would be better*, a thought that luckily hadn't jumped out of his mouth.

She folded her arms beneath her breasts. "You're not going to ask me to be one of your ranch hands, are you?"

He couldn't stop a laugh. "Not hardly. Just trying to be hospitable."

"Oh. You said earlier you wanted to talk to me about business, so I assumed maybe that's why I'm here."

Obviously she wanted to get right down to it. Normally that would suit him fine, but this proposition would take some time easing into it. "We'll cover that in a minute. First, I want you to officially meet Raven."

She looked almost alarmed. "Is that necessary? I mean, he is rather big."

He crossed the aisle and took her hand. "He's big all right. A big baby. He won't hurt you."

"Are you sure?" she asked, a good dose of wariness in her voice.

"Positive."

He guided her to the gelding's stall, stood behind her and told her, "Just pet him on his muzzle."

"Huh?"

"His nose. Or rub him right between his eyes on that white part, which is known as a blaze. He'll follow you anywhere if you do that."

She glanced back at him and frowned. "I'm not sure I want him following me."

"Give it a try, darlin'. You'll see he's a gentle giant. Besides, if you're serious about going on that cattle drive, you better get used to being around a horse before you climb on his back."

After a moment's hesitation, Paris reached out and touched Raven carefully, then slowly began to stroke him. The gelding didn't move an inch, as predicted, and soon began to close his eyes like he'd been hypnotized. Dallas, on the other hand, began to twitch as he followed her movements and imagined her hands on him...

He had a dirty mind full of devilish thoughts that

could land him in trouble, or on his ass if he acted on them. To make matters worse, Paris suddenly turned and ended up way too close for his comfort.

He figured it would be best if he continued the tour, but when she wet her lips, he could only move toward her, not away. And this time, he took the reins. He lowered his head and kissed her like he hadn't kissed a woman in years.

The next thing he knew, he had her spun around and backed up against the wall. She had her hands wrapped around his neck and that sweet little body pressed against his. All thoughts of wedding pacts and proposing to a virtual stranger flew out of his brain in lieu of what was going on below his belt.

Without warning, Paris broke the kiss and ducked under his arm. "This should not be happening."

Dallas braced both palms on the wall and tipped his forehead against the wood. "Maybe not, but it did. Too late to take it back."

"I wish I could take it back," she said from behind him. "I don't understand what is wrong with me. I see no reason whatsoever why I keep acting this way."

That ticked him off a bit and turned him around to face her. "Are you going to try to ignore the chemistry between us? Because I'm sure as hell not going to even try. From the minute you marched into the office, I knew something was brewing."

She looked away for a few seconds. "It's immaterial whether we share chemistry or not. I've made it a point not to do anything rash, and I'm not inclined to sleep with someone outside a committed relationship."

Hell, not only was she sexy, she could read minds. "I don't remember asking you to sleep with me."

She sent a pointed look south of his buckle. "You might not have verbally asked, but the message was loud and clear."

That wasn't up for discussion. "Hey, I'm a man. We don't always have control over physical reactions."

She gave him a good eye-rolling. "That could be true, but I do have control over mine."

"Lady, you could've fooled me a few minutes ago. And don't forget that kiss last night."

"Evidently I forgot myself."

"Maybe you've just forgotten what it feels like to be with a man who really wants you."

Her indignant look told him he'd struck a nerve. "Look, I have a few rules. I don't believe in casual sex, and I don't become intimate with anyone I've known such a short time. Never have. Never will."

A good lead-in to his crazy scheme, *crazy* being the operative word. But for the first time in a long time, he saw a possible end to his dilemma. Not to mention being married to Paris Reynolds carried a couple of perks, the least of which would be some nice, hot lovemaking. First, he had to convince her to give his plan credence.

He paced down the aisle and back again before he paused in front of her. "No sex outside a committed relationship, huh?"

"That is correct."

He rubbed a palm over his neck and prepared to propose. "Then if that's the case, I can only see one answer to the problem."

"What would that be?"

"Marry me."

Four

"Have you lost your mind?"

"Nope."

Paris found it difficult to believe a man like Dallas Calloway—a reputed confirmed bachelor—would blurt out a proposal to a woman he'd known less than twenty-four hours. "Let me get this straight. You'd be willing to marry me in order to sleep with me?"

"Yep."

This simply had to be a joke with an impending punch line. "Shouldn't we go steady first?"

"I'm serious, Paris, and I'm not asking just so I can get you into my bed."

From the somber look on his face, she could tell he was dead serious. "If it's not only the sex, then why would you want to rush into a marriage?"

"Because I need a wife and I need one fairly fast."

Her head started spinning from confusion. "Could you be any more vague?"

"It's kind of complicated. But I believe getting married would benefit both of us."

In what universe? "This doesn't make any sense to me, Dallas. As I said before, you could probably have any woman you wanted and—"

"I don't want any other woman. And in all honesty, I'm running out of time to find a bride."

Paris entertained visions of gloom and doom. "Is there something physically wrong with you?"

"Do you mean a terminal illness?"

"Yes."

"No, but I am suffering from an incurable codicil."

"Now I'm really perplexed."

"Join the club." He gestured toward the end of the lengthy barn. "Let's go into the office. You're going to need to sit down while I explain."

That sounded like a good plan. Her knees were still weak from their mini make-out session and the bombshell proposal. "Lead the way."

Paris followed Dallas into the office that was surprisingly simple and blessedly cool. She took a black-and-chrome chair situated in the corner while he leaned back on the industrial metal desk opposite her.

Dallas released a rough sigh as he centered his gaze on her. "Before I launch into this mess, I need to know I can trust you with the information I'm about to disclose."

She braced for deep secrets, an all too familiar concept. "I promise I won't say anything. Besides, I really don't have anyone to tell, at least not around here. And I promise you I have no intention of mentioning any of this conversation to my mother and father."

"No best friend?"

"Not really. I basically lost touch with my friends from college." A sad commentary on the state of her life.

"Good, because some of my current predicament involves a scandal."

Her curiosity was considerably piqued. "Go ahead."

After looking away a few moments, Dallas finally regarded her again. "A few years ago, during the reading of my dad's will, we discovered he had another family we didn't know a damn thing about."

"You mean Jenny?"

"Yeah, and the twins."

Both shocking and scandalous. "I didn't realize your dad and Maria divorced."

"They didn't."

The cogs started spinning in her head as she added outrageous to the adjectives describing the situation. "You mean he was—"

"A bigamist."

"How did he get away with that?"

"By leaving the state to screw around on Maria. He bought a horse farm in Louisiana when Maria was pregnant with my half brother Houston. He met Jenny in New Orleans, married her and proceeded to get her pregnant not long after my other half brother Tyler was born. For over twenty years he lived the lie and no one was the wiser."

Paris felt as if she'd been thrust into a spaghetti Western soap opera. "I can't imagine keeping a secret of that magnitude for weeks, much less decades."

"J. D. Calloway was a conniving, cheating, lying son of a bitch," he said, venom in his voice. "Pardon my French."

She couldn't believe he would be concerned about cursing in light of what he'd just told her. "No worries. My father speaks the language fluently."

Her attempt at humor obviously fell flat when Dallas didn't even crack a smile. "But that part of the sorry story isn't even the worst of it."

Paris had a difficult time believing it could get much worse. Then again… "Please don't tell me he had another wife."

"Not that we're aware of, although I wouldn't put it past him. But he did have it out for me."

"Why is that?"

"Because he never could control me in life, so he decided to do it in death."

She definitely didn't think she'd care for the late Calloway patriarch. "How exactly did he manage that?"

"By using ownership of the ranch. He knew my grandfather insisted the controlling interest of the D Bar C be passed down to his first-born grandson, and my dad was forced to adhere to that request. But then he added a condition that would allow me to continue to run this place only if I did his bidding."

She was almost afraid to ask. "Such as?"

"I have to get married before my thirty-eighth birthday. If not, controlling interest reverts to my half brother Fort who doesn't give a tinker's damn about this place. He's so ate up with anger he'd like to see all of us fail."

So now she knew why that milestone held so much importance with the mothers. And she suspected she knew the reason behind the spontaneous proposal. "Am I correct in assuming you want me to prevent that from happening by entering into a bogus marriage?"

He scowled. "When you put it that way, it makes me sound like a jerk. But after I met you yesterday and learned about your current situation, I figured it would benefit us both."

"How am I going to benefit from a lie?"

"Financially."

She'd begun to feel a bit like the prostitute Maria had believed her to be. "Marriage for money. Interesting. And out of the question."

"Will you at least hear me out?"

"I wouldn't miss it for the world. But first, I have to know one thing."

"Go ahead."

"How could you put that much faith in this plan when you know so little about me?"

He paused for a brief moment. "Your parents are Howard and Sheila Reynolds. You were born in San Diego thirty-two years ago on November second. You graduated from a prestigious college, worked for an equally prestigious firm in Nevada and you married Peter L. Smith in Vegas eight years ago. I didn't find any record of your divorce though."

She was floored he'd gained so much information in such a short time. "I have the documents although they're in Spanish, and a photo of the book where the registrar recorded the divorce. And exactly when did you do this background check on me?"

"I couldn't sleep last night so I did an internet search. This morning I called a friend who's in security. He took it from there."

Security meant criminal history. Momentary panic set in. "Did he find anything interesting?"

"Nope. Not one felony or misdemeanor or even a speeding ticket."

She relaxed for a moment knowing he hadn't discovered her primary secret, but then no one knew about that. No one ever would, thanks to a nondisclosure order arranged by her attorney. "I'd expect you to thoroughly investigate someone you intend to hire, but not someone you intend to marry."

"I'm a businessman, Paris, and this is a business proposition. Maybe that sounds kind of crass, but before we go any further, I wouldn't want you to have expectations of it being anything else."

For some odd reason that stung like a hornet, as if she was stupid enough to think it might be more. "Really? Again I ask, what's in it for me? Aside from being wed to the object of many a woman's lust, of course."

He didn't seem affected at all by her sarcasm. "First of all, you have a fairly substantial debt you're dealing with."

Had he somehow discovered the money she owed

her former firm? Impossible. Or so she hoped. "Did you run a report on my finances?"

"No. I figured that out when you came begging for a job, and confirmed it when you mentioned your ex taking your money and cutting out of the country. I also recall some issue with staying in your apartment and possibly having to move to Idaho. Am I wrong?"

If he only knew the true magnitude of her problems. "No, you're not wrong."

"Exactly how much debt are you carrying?"

"That's really none of your—"

"Business? If you want me to help you, you'll have to be honest about the money aspects."

He had a lot of nerve making the request when she hadn't agreed to anything. "I believe I asked you for a job, not for your help."

"Yeah, but I'm asking for yours. We could help each other. How much debt?"

She momentarily swallowed her pride. "Over seventy thousand dollars." Most of which she owed to her former firm.

"Are you a chronic shopper?" he asked.

"No, but my ex is. He left me with all the bills." Including money he'd stolen that she was having to reimburse.

"Okay. If you agree to this, I'll make sure you're debt-free. I'll give you twenty thousand up front and you can live here rent-free. You can also design the lodge and I'll pay you monthly for that. If you see that through, I'll provide a reference and the seed money to start your own company."

Wow. She would finally be solvent, liberated from her former employer and on her way to a bright future. But at what cost? A nagging voice told her to go for it. Her mother's voice told her to proceed with caution. "If I did agree to this, and I'm not saying I am, how long would I be expected to remain in this marriage?"

"The will states a year," he said. "It's going to take at least that long to get Texas Extreme up and running and the lodge ready for guests. If you'll stay until then, I'll throw in another bonus. I'll buy you a new car so you can put that rusty sedan out to pasture."

She took offense to him insulting her car. "Bubba is not rusty."

He chuckled. "You gave that clunker a name?"

"Yes. He's been very reliable, unlike most men I've known."

"Bubba sounds like he's barely running."

"He does need a little work." Now for a very pertinent question. "There is the very important matter of dissolving the marriage. I'm personally not keen on being labeled a two-time loser with another divorce."

"We could look into an annulment."

"Under what grounds after we've hung in there for a year?"

He streaked a palm over his shaded jaw. "I'm not sure."

Neither was she, but she intended to find out. "Mind if I borrow your laptop to do a little research?"

He reached behind him and offered her the computer. "Knock yourself out."

After setting it on her lap, Paris began the search

for annulment criteria. She selected the most official-looking article and began to read. "Let's see here. The first condition states the parties are family members, but I highly doubt we're related to each other."

"Did you not pay attention to me telling you about my father's philandering ways? I wouldn't be surprised to discover you're the sister I've always wanted but never had."

"Very funny and kind of creepy."

"I'm kidding, Paris. I don't harbor any brotherly feelings for you whatsoever."

She looked up to see Dallas's smile before scanning the text again. "On to the next point. I guess one of us could get drunk during the ceremony and claim we weren't coherent enough to consent. We could then say we didn't sober up until after our first anniversary."

His low laugh gave her pleasant chills. "Sounds like you could handle that with a couple of Jen's mint juleps, pre-ceremony. I'm sure she'll keep you supplied for the next twelve months."

This time she didn't bother to look up. "Clever, but not anything either of us should consider. Coercion is out because I wouldn't agree to this unless we're both sure. Bigamy is also out. And fraud unless one of us is lying about our age."

"Nope," he said. "But back to that bigamy thing. Are you sure you're divorced?"

Realizing she'd inadvertently hit a nerve bringing up bigamy, Paris closed the computer and frowned. "Yes, I'm sure I'm divorced. Peter couldn't get out of the marriage quick enough. He's a CPA so he's fastidious and detail oriented." As well as a con artist, a fact she chose to withhold. "That leaves us with the final possibility. Do you have issues with impotence that would lead to the old standby, failure to consummate?"

He looked more amused than insulted. "You and I both know the answer to that after what happened a few minutes ago."

She'd realized very quickly he hadn't been poking fun. "That's too bad since it would make the whole failure to consummate much easier, which appears to be our only option. Get married, no whoopee."

He looked like he'd just bitten into a dill pickle. "You expect me to go without sex for a year?"

Paris thought that would be the greatest challenge of all, and a possible reason for him to rescind the offer. "Cowboy up, cowboy. You can handle it if you want to keep the ranch. Which leads me to another question."

"Shoot."

"Does maintaining control of this place mean so much to you that you would enter into a fake marriage that requires celibacy for a year?"

"I don't like the celibacy clause one damn bit, but I can only promise I'll try. And it would have to be a real marriage in order to meet the will's requirements."

She saw a possible alternative. "Who would know if we only pretended we married?"

"Fort will make a point to check it out."

The decision would be so much easier for Paris if that weren't the case. "You're obviously a rich guy, Dallas. I imagine you could buy a ranch just like this one anywhere in the world. Maybe even a bigger and better ranch. Then you wouldn't have to resort to this ruse."

"It wouldn't be the same," he said. "To risk sounding like Jenny, the D Bar C is equivalent to losing the plantation that's been in the family for generations."

"Wouldn't it still be in the family if Fort takes over? Have you even bothered to work out some agreement that wouldn't force you to go to such extremes?"

Anger flashed in his eyes. "Fort doesn't talk to anyone but Worth. He'd have the power to do anything he pleases, including selling it off piece by piece. I wouldn't put it past him to do that just for spite. He hates anything associated with the Calloways, including me. Especially me."

A family feud of grand proportions. "Because I grew up traveling the world, I've never experienced having a real home place. But I do understand why it would be difficult to give up a legacy."

"And even harder to give up the memories."

"Of your dad?"

"Of my mother. I have very few as it is."

That revelation yanked hard on her heartstrings. At times her own mother could drive her insane with her penchant for being overprotective, yet Paris couldn't imagine not having her mom in her life. "How old were you when she passed?"

"Not quite five years old, but I still recall the little things. If I'm forced to leave here, I'm afraid the memories might fade completely."

Hearing the pain in his voice almost pushed Paris over the marriage edge. But she couldn't let emotions rule common sense. She'd done that too often as it was. "You've given me a lot to consider," she said as she handed him the laptop.

"Then you're not completely ruling it out?"

"No, but I have to think about it long and hard. And you'd have to promise we'd find some way to go the annulment route."

"Believe me, my lawyer will find a loophole if that's how we want to end the marriage. And I'd be willing to put all the terms in writing if that would make you feel better."

She'd feel better if she had more time to weigh the verdict. "When do you want my answer?"

"I'm flying to Houston on Friday and I thought we could just do it there. It'll be easier to blend in at that courthouse rather than do it around here. Word travels fast in small towns."

"I don't know if I can make such a serious decision that soon."

"That's all the time I have since my birthday's Saturday," he said as he pushed off the desk. "When it comes right down to it, it makes sense to get it done the day before."

If only she could be so sure. "I'm going to go home and think it over," she told him as she stood. "But if I were you, I wouldn't get my hopes up. I'll call you as soon as I've made up my mind."

After leaving him behind in the barn, Paris managed to return to Dallas's house, gather her things and sneak out without being detected. She drove the ninety miles home in a haze, ticking off a mental list of pros and cons. She entered her barren apartment and thought about how she'd hoped to settle in a loft downtown, with a view of the River Walk. Yet her budget had only allowed her to rent a one-bedroom in a cookie-cutter complex outside the magic of the city.

Her life had turned into an absolute mess, devoid of security and absent of even a shred of a sincere social life. She had a closet full of expensive shoes and nowhere to wear them, a large stack of unpaid bills, including one that if ignored could take away her freedom, and a solid sense of defeat. But she still had an option—accept Dallas's proposal. What was the worst that could happen? Paris could think of one thing—she might lose her heart to a man who didn't return the sentiment. Again.

Not this time. Not if she approached the proposal as strictly business. She married for love the first time, why not marry for financial gain the second? A lot of people did it. Unfortunately she'd never imagined herself fitting into that mercenary mold. But she'd never dreamed she would be caught in this dire position.

Damn her bad luck. Damn Peter Smith for his criminal acts and betrayal and leaving her to take the fall. Damn Dallas Calloway for putting her on the verge of accepting his offer.

Knowing she needed advice had her reaching for the cell phone, although she would have to be very, very careful.

On that thought, Paris dropped down onto the sofa and pounded out her parents' number. After two rings,

"Reynolds residence" filtered through the line in Sheila's usual sing-song voice.

"Hey, Mom. It's Paris."

"Well I'll be, it's the prodigal daughter checking in and it's not even a holiday."

Her mom did have a tendency to make her kids feel guilty at times. "I know, Mother. It's been a while since I called, but I've been rather busy."

"Do you have a job?"

That depended on whether she took a husband. "Actually, I have a good prospect." Now for adding that other little tidbit of information. "I also have a new man in my life."

"Oh, Paris, are you sure that's a good idea? The ink has barely dried on your divorce decree."

"It's been twenty-two months, Mom." And four days.

"Oh. Time does fly, doesn't it?"

"Yes, it does. Anyway, I think you and Dad would like him."

"Does *he* have a job?"

"Yes, he does. He's a rancher. An honest to goodness cowboy."

"Interesting. Does he have a nice butt?"

Heavens, leave it to her matriarch to bring that up. "What difference does it make?"

"Believe me, it does. I married your father for his butt and we're approaching forty years of marital bliss."

Definitely too much information. "Yes, he has a nice butt and a nice house and a lucrative ranching operation. Are you happy now?"

"I'm happy if you're happy, dear."

Now for the moment of truth. A prelude to what possibly could be in the offing. "Good, because the *M* word has been mentioned."

"Meatloaf? Manners? *Mistake*?"

"Very funny, Mom. Marriage."

"Darn, I'd hoped that wasn't it."

"Nothing is set in stone yet, but I didn't want you to be blindsided if it does happen."

"I certainly hope we get to meet this one before you take that step."

Not likely that would occur in two days. "I'm sure you'll have the opportunity in the near future."

"Paris, if this man treats you well, then you'll have our blessing. Just make certain this time you're doing the right thing."

An obvious slam on her lack of judgment when it came to her former relationship. "Believe me, I'm going to be very certain before I end up at the altar. A part of me says I should go for it. Another part tells me maybe I'm not cut out for matrimony."

"I don't want to ever hear you say that again," her mother said in a no nonsense tone. "You have the capacity to make a marriage work, as long as you can trust and love your mate for life."

Therein lay the problem—love didn't figure into the deal. "How do you ever really know that, Mother? Marriage doesn't come with guarantees."

"True, but it does come with certain risks if it's not right. If you happen to be lucky enough to find your soul mate, then don't be afraid to take the chance. One bad apple named Peter shouldn't spoil the whole bunch. By the way, what is this man's name?"

"Dallas." And sadly he would never be her soul mate, though he could be her financial savior.

"How nice that he carries the moniker of your father's favorite football team. That should earn him a few points."

They shared in a laugh before Paris decided to end the conversation. "Thanks for listening, Mom. I'll take all your advice to heart."

"You're welcome, dear. And don't forget to follow that heart. If it feels right, do it. It's high time to leave the past behind and look forward to a brighter future."

"You know, Mom, you're right. Love you bunches and tell Dad I love him, too."

"We love you, dear. And don't wait so long to call, okay?"

"I won't." And that next call could be a bombshell that might blow up in her face.

After Paris hung up, she mulled over her mother's words and clung to one thing in particular—leaving the past behind and looking forward to a brighter future.

Maybe she should choose a different direction, journey down a new path, even an unorthodox one. Maybe marriage to Dallas Calloway could provide all of that, and more. Maybe his offer would be the best way to start over.

Too much to consider, and far too little time.

Right then, Dallas only wanted enough time to enjoy his lunch alone. But the two women hovering at the dinette where he now sat had no intention of giving him some peace. Maybe if he ignored them, they'd go away. And pigs would probably sprout wings first.

Jenny propped one hand on her hip and stared at him. "Well?"

He swallowed the last bite of the barbecue sandwich before he responded. "Well what?"

"Where is Paris?"

"She went home."

Maria flipped her braid over one shoulder and folded her arms. "Are you gonna ask her out again, *mijo*?"

"Nope."

Jenny sighed. "Sugar, you really should have given her another chance. A lot of women get drunk on a first date."

He saw an opportunity to rattle their chains and jumped on it. "I decided I didn't need to ask her for a second date."

Jen looked crestfallen. "Why not?"

"Because I asked her to marry me. I figured we'd pretty much moved past the dating game at that point."

That effectively shut them up for the time being, but he suspected not for long.

"You really did it?" Jenny asked, confirming his suspicions.

"Yeah, I did."

"Don't just sit there, *mijo*," Maria said. "Give us all the down and dirty details."

Jenny took on that same old wistful, romantic look. "Did you get down on one knee? Did you give her a ring?"

That beat all he'd ever heard. "No, I didn't get down on one knee. I approached it as a business proposition, which it is. And when would I have found time to buy a ring?"

"You have your mother's ring, Dallas. It's in the safe."

Maria didn't have to remind him of that. He'd thought about it often, even though he'd never really looked inside the blue velvet box. Giving it to Paris under the circumstances would be as false as the marriage. Ironically, that trinket had been reserved for true love, according to his dad. "A ring is the least of my concerns."

Jenny's face fell like it had weights attached to it. "She said no?"

He pushed back from the table and came to his feet. "She said she'd think about it."

"Then it's not a lost cause?" Maria asked.

"Okay, you two, don't get your hopes up." Exactly what Paris had said to him before she'd left. "My guess is she's going to think it over and then refuse the offer."

"You should have knelt before her," Jenny said. "Women like that."

"And given her the damn ring," Maria added. "I'm not sappy like Blondie here, but I do know most gals like to be treated with dignity when a man pops the question. Even your father knew that."

"That's true," Jenny began. "J.D. could be quite the romantic even if he was a jackass."

He didn't want to hear anything else about the aforementioned jackass since he was the reason Dallas found himself in this predicament. "It wasn't going to matter to Paris if I rode in on a white horse, considering what I'm asking of her."

"A white horse would have been nice," Jenny added. "That would be hard to resist."

He wanted to shake some sense into the woman and dislodge her visions of hearts and flowers. "Again, the ball is now in Paris's court. If she wants to agree to the marriage terms, then she'll let me know."

"Maybe you should go after her," Maria added. "Give her a little nudge in the right direction."

He had actually thought about doing that very thing before deciding he didn't want to pressure her more than he already had. "If she wants to go forward, she'll come to me. I'm not going to coerce her into a decision." Although that would be a reason for ending the marriage, provided it actually happened. Nah. His sense of honor wouldn't allow him to use that tactic.

"I hope she does say yes," Jenny said. "We could plan a grand wedding on the grounds of the main house. I could make canapés and my famous mint juleps."

That's all he needed—a drunk bride. Then again, that would be grounds for the annulment. He really had to get a grip. "If she decides to go through with it, and that's a big *if*, there won't be any wedding. Just a simple courthouse ceremony and no publicity."

Jenny pretended to pout. "That's no fun, Dallas. You should have your family present for the nuptials."

Before she called a caterer, Dallas had to get out of there. "You ladies have a good afternoon talking about me behind my back."

With that, he left the kitchen and headed to the barn,

all the while recalling how he'd watched Paris drive away. Probably for the last time.

In reality, the marriage pact was the craziest thing he'd ever conjured up. He sure as hell couldn't imagine keeping his hands to himself for a day in her presence, much less a year. If everything fell through, he'd be better off. He'd just turn the place over to Fort and find somewhere else to start up Texas Extreme, even if it wouldn't be the same.

Accepting the fact that Paris would turn him down flat would be best. He'd bet his last buck that's exactly what she'd do.

Five

"With the power vested in me by the state of Texas, I now pronounce you husband and wife."

The man should probably be pronouncing them certifiably insane. Four days ago she hadn't even known Dallas Calloway. Two days ago she'd packed up her limited belongings and moved in with him. Today she wore a diamond-encrusted wedding band and vowed to be his wife. Unbelievable.

Paris waited for Dallas to follow the justice of the peace's declaration, expecting a peck on the cheek. Perhaps a brush across her mouth. She got a full-on, well-deep kiss that curled her toes in the white satin pumps she'd purchased with the sleeveless matching dress before she'd left San Antonio.

After Dallas pulled away and winked, she automatically touched her tingling lips. "That certainly sealed the deal."

He leaned over and whispered, "There's more of that to come if you want more of it."

Yes, she wanted more. Much more than she should. "Now that we've made this official, what's the next step?"

"I have a driver waiting outside the north entrance. He'll take us back to the plane."

The private plane that had whisked her to Houston a few hours ago to meet up with the groom following his appearance at the grand opening of his newest saddle shop. An elaborate aircraft that could pass for a flying motel with a high-class bar and sleeping quarters, of all things.

Dallas clasped her hand to guide her through the courthouse vestibule and when they stepped outside, Paris was shocked to find hoards of reporters milling around the steps outside. "What is going on?"

"They're here for us," Dallas muttered, followed by a few strong oaths. "Just keep walking and stay close to me."

"Not a problem." She had no intention of crawling into the lion's den without a proper escort.

As soon as they started their descent, cameras immediately began to flash, film began to roll and some woman with red hair as big as Jenny's started hurling questions at Paris. "How does it feel to be married to one of the most eligible bachelors in the state?" she asked as she thrust a microphone in Paris's face.

Before she could respond, Dallas practically dragged

her toward the black limo waiting at the curb as he shoved his way through the crowd. She could swear someone tugged at the hem of her dress right before the chauffeur helped her into the car and away from the chaos.

Dallas slid in bedside her and immediately began to loosen his tie. "Dammit, I wanted to avoid all this nonsense. I'd like to know who the hell tipped them off."

"That's anyone's guess. Maybe someone in the courthouse when you obtained our marriage license. By the way, how did you manage to circumvent the normal waiting period?"

He shrugged out of his beige jacket and laid it on the seat beside him. "I know people. Obviously people that can't be trusted."

She imagined he did know a lot of people in high places. She also imagined him taking off the white tailored shirt, his best pair of jeans and cowboy boots, and laying her down on the leather seat. Maybe she'd request he leave the boots on. Maybe she should exit the car now before she found herself in a lot of trouble. As if she wasn't already. "You know, marriages are a matter of public record, Dallas. I'm sure that's how the media learned about us."

"We haven't even been married fifteen minutes. Someone at the courthouse must've leaked the info. Probably an employee who wanted to make a buck selling a story."

Curious over how far the news had traveled, Paris pulled her cell from her silk bag and did a quick internet search of their names. In less than five seconds, she had her answer from a renowned celebrity gossip site. "Oh, my gosh. I can't believe this headline. Sexy Former Rodeo Superstar Dallas Calloway Marries Longtime Girlfriend Paris Reynolds."

"Don't know why you're so shocked," he said with a grin. "Some women think I'm sexy. My truck, too."

He was just too darned cute not to tolerate his wry wit. "I'm referring to the *longtime* part. Talk about a misprint. It should read His Girlfriend of Three Days. Or more accurately, His Business Partner."

He scooted a little closer to her, providing another heady whiff of his clean-scent cologne. "I wouldn't be surprised if they didn't get hold of Jenny for an interview. She'd say something like that to make the situation more socially acceptable."

"I suppose she would do that since she's definitely all about decorum."

"She's also still mad she wasn't invited to witness the wedding. So is Maria." After his cell began to ring, he pulled it from his jeans' pocket and said, "Speak of the devil."

"Which one?"

"Jen."

When he simply stared at the phone, Paris wondered why he was hesitating. "What are you waiting for?"

"I'm tryin' to decide if I want to speak to her."

"Of course you do. It might be an emergency."

"Yeah, her pantyhose could be shot or her hairdresser canceled her appointment."

"Answer it, Dallas."

"Fine." He swiped the screen and grumbled, "What's

up, Jen?" followed by a few *yeahs* and couple of *yeps* and one *big deal*. Then he added, "I'll take that into consideration, and I don't give a horse's rear what he thinks. And yeah, I forgive you but only because he's your kid. Talk to you later."

"What was that all about?" Paris asked after he disconnected.

Dallas forked a hand through his hair and sighed. "It seems Jen decided to call Fort and tell him we were getting married and where. When she saw the story at five a couple of minutes ago—"

"Why does our marriage warrant coverage on the news channels?"

He looked at her as if she'd lost her mind. "She was watching some tabloid channel, not the national news. But be prepared for that to happen. Weddings, babies and divorces of the rich and infamous equal good ratings."

Apparently their surprising little wedding was worthy of major coverage, thanks to the notoriety of the man sitting beside her. The man who happened to legally be her husband. "I knew you were popular with the ladies, but I had no idea losing your bachelor status would have such an impact on the general public."

He shrugged. "No one thought it would ever happen. Anyway, Fort evidently called the press just to piss me off. Jen says a lot of reporters are camped out near the ranch. Maria's doing her best to run them off, hopefully not with a shotgun. Like I suspected, Jen also said it was her idea to claim we've been a couple for a long time."

"How long?"

"Three years, and she's real proud of the plan."

The *plan* could be a major problem. "Unfortunately that would make me an adulteress since I've been divorced less than two years. I hope that doesn't come back to haunt us."

He reached into the built-in cooler centered between the opposing rows of seats and withdrew a bottle of high-dollar champagne. "If it does create problems, we'll deal with it. In the meantime, let's celebrate our nuptials."

Celebrating wasn't foremost on her mind. Not when she continued to worry that somehow someone might dig up the dirt from the debacle at her former firm. But she couldn't concern herself with something that happened to be beyond her control. Besides, if Dallas found out, she'd simply explain she'd only been guilty of being too gullible. "Nice touch," she said after he poured them each a glass of the bubbly and offered one to her. "But I wouldn't peg you as a wine drinker."

"Normally, I'm not, but I think we deserve a toast." He held the glass aloft. "To an arrangement that will allow us to both win in the end."

As long as *the end* didn't include an emotional hijacking, she'd drink to that. "To winning," she said as she touched the flute to his.

After taking a few sips, Paris leaned back in the seat, looked out the window and noticed the slow-moving traffic. "It's going to take forever to get to the airport."

Dallas downed the rest of the champagne and grimaced before setting the glass aside. "That's what happens in Houston during rush hour. Guess we should have planned better."

The situation could work to their advantage. "Since we have the extra time, we should probably use it to get to know each other."

He scooted closer, draped his arm over the back of the seat and grinned. "I'm game."

"I don't mean that." Even though *that* would be tempting.

He slid a fingertip down her cheek. "Are you sure? I mean, we are newlyweds and we're in this big old limo with all this room. The driver can't see a thing with the window up."

More very vivid images filtered into her thoughts. Risqué images that caused her face to fire up. She didn't know whether to fan herself or faint. "I'm referring to discussing details about each other, in case anyone asks. After all, we've presumably been together for three years."

He released a rough sigh. "Talking wasn't what I had in mind."

"Of course not. You're a man. You're averse to conversation."

He traced a random pattern on her knee. "Not always. Just at the moment."

She slapped her palm on his hand and placed it on the seat between them, even though she considered sliding it up her thigh. "Now, now. Be a good groom. We both know the terms."

"I don't like the terms one damn bit."

In reality, neither did she. But she liked the thought

of another divorce even less. "First get-to-know-you question. What's your favorite color?"

"Brown. Yours?"

"Coral. Favorite pastime?"

"I thought I made that clear right before you threw the no-sex terms up in my face."

Definitely a bad boy. "Your second favorite then."

"Taking a long, hard ride on a—"

"Dallas," she said in a scolding tone.

"Bull." He tried on an innocent look that didn't quite erase the devilish gleam in his blue eyes. "What did you think I was going to say?"

The man knew exactly what she'd been thinking, and with good reason. "Moving on. Favorite food?"

"Steak."

She knew the answer to that before she'd asked the question. "I love hummus with red peppers."

He frowned. "I'd rather eat hay. Your favorite vacation spot?"

"I haven't been on a vacation in so long I couldn't really say. I do know it's not Vegas. I've seen enough of that place to last a lifetime."

"Never been a big fan," he said. "Except when I was at the National Finals Rodeo. Now that I've retired, give me a fishing trip any day."

"I've never been fishing," she said.

"Never?"

"No. My father spent his career on boats so he avoided taking us anywhere that involved water."

Dallas remained quiet for a while before he asked, "How would you feel about going fishing?"

"Today?"

"Sure. We've got to spend our honeymoon somewhere, not to mention the press is hanging out at the ranch, waiting for our return. We could just kick back a couple of days. I can teach you how to cast a line and we can just relax."

Had this been a traditional marriage, she might have preferred a tropical paradise in lieu of a fishing excursion. However, that fit Dallas's cowboy persona, not consuming fruity drinks with umbrellas during an island escape. Avoiding any more media coverage for the time being sounded like a good idea no matter where they went. She did see one problem. "I didn't pack a bag, Dallas."

"Just leave it all up to me. I promise you'll have everything you need."

She trusted he would make good on that promise. "Okay. Exactly where will we go?"

"Lady, this is your lucky day. I just happen to know this little cabin on a lake."

It had to be the biggest log cabin she'd ever seen.

When they'd arrived at the airport an hour ago, they'd been greeted by a fiftysomething-year-old man who'd delivered Dallas a tricked-out black truck, complete with leather seats, satellite radio and a high-tech computer. They'd immediately set off for Texas Hill Country, northwest of San Antonio, luggage on board as promised, for their impromptu honeymoon. And now they traveled up a steep drive lined by a myriad of trees toward another magnificent property.

"This place is really yours?" Paris asked as Dallas pulled into the circular drive and stopped before the front door.

He turned off the ignition and gave her a prideful smile. "Yep. I helped build it with my own two hands a couple of years ago. It's a nice place to escape, although I don't get to enjoy it often enough. Now wait right here."

After undoing her seat belt, Paris remained in her seat while Dallas rounded the hood and helped her out. He only let go of her hand to open the pine door, and then caught her completely off guard when he picked her up into his arms.

She had a little trouble catching her breath as he stepped inside. "What on earth are you doing, Dallas?"

"Carrying my bride over the threshold."

Even her *official* first husband hadn't done that. "Isn't this a bit of overkill considering our situation?"

"The caretaker doesn't know our situation," he said as he set her on her feet atop the wood plank floors. "And I don't know if he's left yet. I'm going to check the place over then I'll bring in the bags."

After Dallas left her alone to her devices, Paris readjusted her dress and tightened the band at her nape. The man had literally swept her off her feet. Imagine that. If not careful, she might actually start viewing him as a real husband. Not wise at all.

Pushing the concerns aside, she surveyed the great room with floor-to-towering-ceiling windows that afforded a view of the wooded terrain. Or what she could see of it now that the sun had disappeared. The place was rustic, like its owner, but charming all the same. Most of the accent pieces appeared to be antiques, with a lot of Western art and bronze statues. The heavy wood furniture with tufted cushions could have been hand-made, and the decor most likely had been strictly se-lected by Dallas. She could also tell it wasn't nearly as large as his ranch house, but just as masculine if not more so. In fact, she saw no evidence whatsoever of a woman's touch.

A few minutes later, Dallas came back through the front door, toting the suitcases, and startling her sense-less. "All clear."

"How did you manage to sneak by me?"

He set the suitcases down by the oversize sectional. "I went out the back door then walked around to the front."

Logical, though she couldn't lay claim to much logic of late. "Oh. Makes sense."

He pointed to his left. "Kitchen and dining room are in there, along with the back door." He then pointed to his right. "Bedrooms are that way. All have their own private bath. You can pick whichever one you want."

"Which one is yours?"

He cracked a crooked grin. "I was hoping you'd pick that one."

Apparently he didn't intend to give up on the sex thing very easily. "You and I both know that's not a good idea, sleeping in the same bed."

"I know no such thing. I think it's a great idea. That way if someone comes calling, we'll at least appear to be the happy couple."

Stubborn man. "Do you routinely have people randomly show up in your bedroom?"

He rubbed his chin and looked as if he had to think about that. "Maybe a time or two back when I was a teen and managed to sneak a girl into my bedroom. But I'm fairly sure Maria isn't going to make a trip down here for that. In fact, she would expect us to be sharing a bed. Jenny, too."

"Do they not know the terms of this marriage?"

"Not exactly, but they do know me."

She had begun to know him, too. She'd also begun to realize resisting him would prove to be a major challenge. "Humor me and show me to my own room, okay?"

He gave her that little boy shrug. "Okay. But this isn't like any honeymoon I've ever read about."

This wasn't like any marriage she'd ever heard of, either. "You'll survive."

"Maybe, but I will be walking funny."

"Ha, ha."

She shadowed Dallas's steps as he led her into a hallway, bags in hand, and stopped at the first open door. "This is probably the smaller of the three, but I think it suits you."

Paris stepped into the room to find the four-poster queen bed draped in an orange-and-white cowhide. "I refuse to sleep with a dead animal."

Dallas chuckled behind her. "It's not real, just made to look that way."

She turned around and scowled. "It's not very tasteful."

"It's my taste. Get used to it. Are you hungry?"

Not anymore. "The little vegetable sandwiches they served us on the plane will tide me over. Right now I'd like to get these shoes off and get into something more comfortable."

"Need any help with that?"

"No, but I do need my suitcase."

He laid her bag on a bench at the foot of the bed. "Lady, you seem to be lacking in the fun department."

"And you seem to have an overabundance of testosterone."

"That I do, and I won't apologize for it."

"I wouldn't dream of asking for an apology." She brushed past him and unzipped the case, only to find some skimpy barely-there bright red nightie. "Who packed this?"

He leaned over her shoulder, his warm breath filtering over her neck. "I'd guess Jenny. She wants to make sure the groom is happy."

"I'm never going to wear this, you know."

He slid his arms around her and whispered, "Stranger things have happened."

She couldn't argue with that. This whole marriage pact was incredibly strange. The butterflies in her tummy were stranger, still. She couldn't recall the last time she'd been so sexually charged she wanted to jump out of her own skin. Or jump into bed with a man she barely knew. Easy. Never.

For her own protection, Paris wrested away from Dallas and strode to the door. "Now run along like a good boy, and take your suitcase with you."

He headed toward her, a determined look on his face.

"They're both yours. I have everything I need in my bedroom. Almost everything."

She didn't have to ask what he meant by that. "Before you go, is it safe to take a walk before bed?"

"Sure. Go out the back door and you'll find a path to the lake."

"Is it well lit?"

"The moon is full tonight. That's enough light for you to see where you're going. Just don't fall into the water. And watch out for snakes."

She cringed. "Snakes?"

He had the gall to grin. "Just kidding. The cats keep them away."

"Cats?"

"Yeah. Big ones. Attack cats. But they've been trained not to bother pretty girls."

With that, he exited, closing the door behind him, leaving Paris alone to unpack, and ponder how she would find the strength of will to ignore his overtures, and her own needs.

She returned to the suitcases, thankful to find something other than naughty negligees in the mix. In the smaller one, Jenny had packed every toiletry known to womankind, and enough underwear to last two months, not two days. The woman had also packed jeans and a few T-shirts, and from those Paris picked her favorite coral knit top and pair of seen-better-days denim with a slash above the right knee, a small hole on the inside of her left thigh, and a pocket that was barely hanging on. That suited her current state of mind.

After exchanging her formal dress for comfort, she

kicked out of her heels and donned the slide-on sneakers that had been stashed in a side pocket. Now she felt more human, if not more calm. Too bad they'd left the champagne in the limo.

She didn't need alcohol, she needed some peace and quiet. Time alone to reflect. With that in mind, she headed into the hall and located the well-equipped kitchen—which was almost as nice as the one back at the ranch—then made her way out the back door.

Dallas had been right about the moon. It cast the manicured lawn in an amber glow and helped guide Paris down the dirt path toward a copse of trees. Fortunately someone had had the foresight to cut a wide clearing in the woods, otherwise she might have been hesitant to continue. A few yards away she could see the shimmering lake and headed in that direction, all the while aware of the sounds of nature, including what sounded like an owl. She managed to make it to the dock without stepping on a critter or coming upon the attack cats.

Once there, she strolled to the end of the pier and lowered herself onto the wooden slats, then hugged her knees to her chest. A slight breeze blew across her face, bringing with it the pleasant scent of cedar. She heard the sound of chirping and an occasional rustle of leaves, which might have unnerved her if she would have still been walking.

On afterthought, she rolled up her jeans, took off her shoes and dangled her feet in the water that was much colder than she'd predicted. But after a while she acclimated to the temperature change and rocked back on her elbows to study the host of stars in the night sky.

For the first time that day, she experienced true tranquility. A sense of well-being as she soaked her sore feet in silence.

"Mind if I join you?"

Paris gasped and nearly vaulted right into the water. She shifted around, palm against her pounding heart, to find Dallas standing above her. "Jeez, you scared me to death!"

He sat beside her without waiting for an invitation and draped his arms on bent knees. "Did you think I was a snake? Or maybe one of the tomcats. Just so you know, they don't talk."

"You startled me because I wasn't expecting you."

"Next time I'll whistle."

Like that would help her anxiety over being accosted by random wildlife. "I'm surprised I didn't hear you."

"No kidding. This dock creaks like box springs on an old iron bed."

No real shock he would bring up a bed analogy. "I was very deep in thought."

"About?"

"Today. This whole thing seems so surreal."

He shifted slightly, leading Paris to believe maybe he was suffering from bride remorse. "Yeah, I know. Never thought it would happen to me."

Her conjecture could very well be right. She wouldn't know what might be on his mind unless she asked. "So what brings you here, other than this bizarre situation?"

"I owe you an apology."

That she hadn't expected. "For what?"

"I'm sorry for coming on too strong. But I won't apologize for wanting you so badly I ache."

She'd never felt so flattered in her life. "Apology accepted, and I'd be telling one colossal lie if I said I wasn't extremely attracted to you. But—"

"But what?" He gave her a meaningful look. "If you're worried about the whole annulment thing, I won't tell if you won't."

"I won't lie under oath. And I have a feeling your integrity won't allow that either."

His sigh cut through the silence. "You're right about that. One thing I learned from my father, deception takes no prisoners. I do think we can find other ways to answer our needs."

Was he suggesting an open marriage? "If you're going to ask if you can see other women, that's your call, but rest assured I wouldn't feel right seeing other men."

"I'm not saying that at all," he said. "We can explore each other without going beyond the limits."

"You mean only foreplay?"

"You got it, darlin'. It's my favorite kind of play."

The thought of his hands on her made her shiver in a very nice way. "That would certainly be new and different for me."

He frowned. "Your husband wasn't into foreplay?"

The understatement of the millennium. "Let me sum up our sex life in a few words. Hi, Paris, just passing through, only have a minute, got to go, see you later. That happened about once a week unless he wasn't in the mood. He always said I was too uptight about my body, but what did he expect when all he did was criticize me?"

"Why in the hell were you with that ass?"

The sheer anger in his voice took her aback. "I was young and stupid. He was my first lover and the first man who really paid attention to me. At least in the beginning. When I got him hired on at the firm, everything changed. I'm fairly certain he cheated on me, although I didn't have any proof. Eventually I didn't even care."

Dallas let go a litany of curses. "You're damn special, Paris. You deserve to be treated that way. And if you want me to show you how good it can be between a man and a woman, all you have to do is ask."

When he rose to his feet, Paris realized she didn't want him to leave. "Where are you going?"

"To grab a snack, take a cold shower and then head to bed."

"Could you stay a little longer?"

"I could, but being so close to you and not being able to touch you is killing me."

She recognized the risk she'd be taking, but she truly craved his attention because she knew with all her heart he would treat her with respect. "I want you to touch me, Dallas. I *need* you to touch me."

He stood statue still and after a few moments asked, "Are you sure?"

She held her hand toward him. "If you'll help me up, I'll go back to the house with you."

"No need for that."

Paris had no idea what he planned to do next when he, too, rolled up his jeans, sat back down, pulled off his socks and boots, then positioned himself behind her, his legs on either side of her thighs. Right at that moment, Paris felt something at her feet beneath the water and gasped again.

"Just relax sweetheart," he told her as he pulled the band away, pushed her hair aside and kissed the back of her neck.

"It's not you. Something was nibbling on my toes."

His slow laugh sent pleasurable chills down her spine. "Darlin', I can do that, but you'll have to wait until it's warmer or until you have your feet out of the lake."

She smiled back at him. "You mean you wouldn't jump in the water if I asked you?"

"Not unless you're waiting for me, naked."

Interesting concept, albeit not logical. "We probably should put that on hold for a couple of months."

"It's a deal."

He kissed her then, thoroughly, stroking her tongue softly with his in a heady rhythm that made her want to climb all over him. If she reacted so strongly to this simple show of affection, she couldn't imagine what she would do if he did anything else.

She would soon find out, she realized, when he broke the kiss and rested his cheek against her cheek, reached beneath her shirt and unclasped her bra. For a moment she felt like a schoolgirl making out with her first real boyfriend in a backseat, an experience she'd never really had. But when Dallas tugged the tee up over her head, taking the bra with it, she knew she was in the hands of a real man. Naked from the waist up. In wide-open spaces.

She should be mortified over being so exposed, but she honestly didn't care. She should have been self-conscious when Dallas whispered, "Watch," but instead she waited with excited anticipation. And the minute he began to circle her nipples simultaneously with his fingertips, she grew hotter than blazes in places still unseen.

As much as she wanted to continue to see what Dallas was doing, Paris closed her eyes and leaned back against him to savor the sensations.

"Feel good?" he asked, his voice low and grainy.

"Yes."

When Dallas slid his palm down her belly, Paris held her breath. And when he began to toy with the button on her jeans, she automatically tensed.

"Just tell me to stop and I will."

She frankly hoped he kept right on going, but then he suddenly halted everything, much to her disappointment. She opened her eyes and stared at him blankly. "I didn't say anything."

He moved from behind her, rolled down his jeans, put on his boots then stood. "I think that's enough for tonight."

She snatched the discarded shirt and clutched it to her bare breasts. "I don't understand."

"Put your shirt on and I'll walk you to the house."

Somewhat miffed, Paris slid the tee over her head,

stood and shoved the bra in her back pocket. "I can find my way."

"Are you mad at me?"

"No. I'm mad at myself for falling into your trap. Nothing good could ever come of mixing business with pleasure and in reality, this is a business arrangement as you have reminded me several times."

"Between two consenting adults who have the hots for each other." He had the nerve to wink. "Darlin', a lot of good could come from it, as soon as you realize sometimes you can't control chemistry. Just let me know when you're ready to explore all our options."

"Don't count on that happening," she said to Dallas as he strode away, leaving her alone to wonder why she couldn't resist him. Why she had let him go so far. Why he could so completely splinter her coveted control, and she welcomed it.

He might have caught her in a moment of weakness, but from that point forward, she vowed to reclaim her power. Call all the shots in this sexual game he seemed determined to play. Turn the tables on him. The time had come to shed her insecurities and prove to him— and to herself—that she could be a strong woman capable of going after what she wanted, wisdom be damned. Business be damned. Fact was, she wanted him.

Perhaps she hadn't been born a natural seductress, or acquired any real skills in thirty-two years, but it was never too late to learn. When it came right down to it, celibacy wasn't the least bit fun.

Six

Celibacy sucked swamp water.

Dallas had discovered that recently but learned long ago the lack of merit in a cold shower. He'd taken one anyway at dawn, following one helluva restless night. Afterward, he'd headed to the kitchen, made a strong pot of coffee, a couple of scrambled eggs and ate them at the kitchen island like he did every morning at the cabin. But his normal news catch-up routine had been disrupted by visions of the woman sleeping down the hall. Just the thought of touching Paris again, going further, going all the way, kept him from focusing on the state of the global markets. But he had to remember the annulment terms—no sex in the real sense.

If he had any hope of maintaining his sanity for the next twelve months, he had two options—take care of the problem himself, or convince Paris they should take care of each other, even if it meant not fully consummating the marriage. He liked the second plan best. Taking it slow seemed to be the only way to accomplish that goal, even though it would damn sure prove to be real hard. Literally. Now if he'd been a dishonorable jerk, he would've crawled into bed with her last night to solve the problem, knowing he'd had her exactly where he'd wanted her before he left her on the dock.

The *problem* only grew more obvious when Paris padded into the room on bare feet, wearing some short flimsy peach-colored robe, her hair piled on top of her head in a messy ponytail. On one hand, she was about as cute as a newborn foal. On the other, she looked sexy as hell, even with her face free of makeup.

She sauntered over to the counter, poured herself a cup of coffee, then turned a sleepy smile on him. "Happy birthday and good morning, handsome husband."

She looked like a birthday gift he wanted to thoroughly investigate. "Mornin', pretty wife." He'd never dreamed those words would ever leave his mouth. But then he'd never imagined meeting anyone like her, either. He liked the way she moved. The way she talked. Her intelligence. Her body. And he knew he would seriously like the way she loved if she gave him the chance to partake of all the benefits that most married couples enjoyed.

Wait a minute. For all intents and purposes, they'd entered into a fabricated union. They weren't playing house, they were doing business. If it was up to her, that's all they'd ever be doing.

Maybe not, he decided, when she sauntered over to the island, sat on the barstool across from him and didn't bother to close the opening of the robe, allowing him a nice view of the curve of her breasts. "Sleep well?"

Not hardly. "Fairly well. And you?"

"You mean after you left me alone topless on the dock? I've had better nights."

"Sorry," he muttered, although he really wasn't all that sorry, except maybe about the leaving part.

She then leaned completely across the granite surface to study the newspaper in front him, causing the robe to gape more and giving him full view of her bare breasts, nipples and all. "*Wall Street Journal*, huh? I expected you to be reading some ranching magazine."

He expected to elevate the island at any moment. "I've been interested in financial news since I acquired my MBA."

Her green eyes went wide as she sat back down, taking his fun away but giving him some moderate relief. "I had no idea you have a graduate degree. Where did you go to school?"

He couldn't resist rattling her chain a little. "Got it online from the University of Dumb Cowpokes."

She laughed softly as she rimmed a fingertip around the coffee cup, drawing Dallas's undivided attention. "Be serious for a change."

He had a serious need to see what else she might be wearing underneath that robe. Or what she wasn't wearing. "I got the undergraduate degree at a small college in Stephenville, Texas, while on a rodeo scholarship. A few years later, when I decided to open the saddle shops, I decided to go for the masters at a bigger university in Fort Worth."

"Impressive. Why saddle shops?"

Recounting his history could calm his rowdy libido. "When I was growing up, a ranch hand named Gordy taught me how to tool roping saddles. I used his design, started my own line of saddles and began to market it."

"Gordy doesn't have a problem with that?"

"Nope. He's happily retired living off the royalties."

"You are a man of many talents, I must say. Do you have any sugar?"

Ignoring the urge to tell her he could give her something really sweet, Dallas nodded toward the cabinet behind her. "Right next to the coffee maker."

She glanced over one shoulder before sending him another smile. "Oh. I didn't see it," she said as she slid out of her chair.

She sure had great legs, he realized, when she walked to the counter to sweeten her coffee. The robe was so short that if she lifted her arms, he felt sure he could see her bottom. He should've told her the canister was in an upper cabinet. He'd give a month's worth of pay to find some excuse for her to bend over. He didn't have to let go of a dime when she dropped the spoon on the floor and reached down to pick it up.

Damn if she didn't have on a thing. Damn if she didn't have one fantastic butt. And damn if he didn't have the mother of all erections.

She turned around and leaned back against the counter. "What are your plans for the day?"

He could offer up a few that involved staying horizontal for the next twenty-four hours, but remembered his aim to take it easy. "I thought we'd go fishing."

She sipped her coffee then set the cup aside. "Sounds like fun. When do you want to do it?"

Right now on the kitchen island. "We need to get going before it gets much later, while the fish are still biting."

"Then I should hurry. What should I wear?"

Not a damn thing. "T-shirt and jeans, I guess. Or shorts. It's going to be close to eighty degrees today."

While Dallas sat there suffering from lack of sex, Paris rinsed her cup out in the sink and put it in the dishwasher, unaware of his predicament. "I'll take a quick shower and be back in a few. Where should I meet you once I'm finished?"

In my bed. Your bed. Any bed. "The dock."

"The dock it is. Maybe I'll just show up without my top to save time."

Taking Dallas totally by surprise, Paris untied the sash at her waist, turned around and let the robe fall from her shoulders onto the floor as she walked away.

The image of her slender back and shapely butt remained burned in his brain long after she disappeared.

Was she just trying to torture him, or give him a taste of his own medicine? He didn't know the answer, but he sure as hell intended to find out.

Paris wondered what effect, if any, her little attempt at seduction had had on Dallas. If he only knew how difficult it had been to completely let go of her inhibitions, then maybe he might have said *something*. When

she'd left him in the kitchen, she hadn't had the forti-
tude to wait around. He certainly hadn't sought her out
in the shower, or showed up at the bedroom door. Only
time would tell what he might have in store for her during their little excursion, and the closer she came to the
dock, the more the excitement escalated.

She discovered him waiting for her, dressed in khaki
cargo shorts and a sleeveless army-green tank, revealing
a pair of very masculine legs and muscled biceps that
sent her heart on a marathon. A few moments passed
before she noticed the sleek silver-and-red boat with the
covered hull tied to the side of the pier.

After sliding her sunglasses into place, Paris stepped
onto the creaky planks and made her way to her tour
guide for the day. "Is this yours?"

"Yep," he replied.

"How did it get here?"

"George."

Clearly he'd decided to be cryptic. "Who is George?"

"My neighbor. He looks after the place when I'm not
here, and in exchange I let him use the boat. I called
and had him deliver it a few minutes ago."

Evidently George wasn't going to join them, a very
good thing. "I see. I've never been on this kind of boat
before. It looks like it costs a pretty penny."

"About eighty grand."

Paris nearly swallowed the gum she'd been chewing. "Eighty thousand dollars? For that price, it should
clean the house, or at least do more than float around
the water looking pretty."

"It can fly," he said as he held out his hand. "If you're lucky, I might let you drive it."

As long as he had sufficient insurance since she'd never been behind the wheel of a boat before. "I might take you up on that, if you're lucky."

He cracked a crooked grin. "I have a feeling we could both be lucky today."

She returned his smile. "Could be." Or not, depending on how far she wanted the seduction scheme to go.

After Dallas helped Paris down into the space-age looking seat, he untied the boat then claimed the space next to her. One hand on the wheel, he backed away from the dock slowly, said, "Hang on," then turned the craft around and shot off into open water.

Yes, the thing could fly, and she couldn't hold a conversation with him due to all the wind noise. She basically clutched the sides of the seats, gritted her teeth and only breathed easier when he navigated the boat into a secluded cove fifteen minutes later.

She pulled away the band securing her high ponytail and finger-combed her hair. "You need to turn around and go back."

He frowned. "Why?"

"Because I think I left my stomach a few miles back."

He barked a laugh. "I take it you're not much of a thrill seeker."

Only partially true. She'd married him on a moment's notice, hadn't she? And she was definitely seeking some thrills today. "I've ridden a few roller coasters on several occasions, but I wasn't quite prepared for this."

Paris *had* prepared to turn on the charms and hopefully turn him on in the process. On that note, she crossed her arms, grabbed the T-shirt's hem and tugged it over her head, leaving her clad in a red bikini top.

Dallas cleared his throat and shut down the ignition. "Didn't know you had a swimsuit."

"Actually, I didn't either," she said as she stood. "Jenny thought of everything." Including massage oil and lubricants, a veritable sex shop in a bag.

"No surprise there," he replied, his voice sounding somewhat grainy.

Paris realized she didn't have a lot of room to maneuver, so she pointed to the enclosed hull. "What's under there?"

"A live well to keep fresh bait and fish and a place to store equipment." He climbed over the smoked glass minidash and stood on the decking to toss an anchor overboard into the murky green water. "You basically turn on the trolling motor and stand here to fish, but we're going to stay stationary until you learn how to cast."

"Or I could sunbathe," she said as she retraced his steps and stood before him. "I can do that while we fish, right?"

"Not a whole lot of sun with all the trees, but whatever floats your boat, pun intended."

She shimmied out of the shorts and tossed them back onto the seat, revealing the scant swimsuit bottoms. "I'm ready for a pole now."

That earned her a wily grin. "I can fix you right up."

"Fishing pole, Dallas."

"I've got one of those, too."

"You have an evil mind."

"You have an unbelievable body."

She felt a head-to-toe blush coming on, and the same old belief he'd simply been trying to be nice. "I bet you say that to all your first mates."

He tucked one side of her hair behind her ear. "You're technically my first mate."

If only she could say the same for herself. If only she could erase Peter from her past and if only this arrangement with Dallas was real. "Well, I suppose we should start fishing before they stop biting."

He stared at her a few moments before leaning over, opening a hatch and pulling out a rod. "I've got this rigged to catch a bass. I also have some blood bait for catfish if you'd prefer to try for one of those."

She wrinkled her nose. "Any bait that includes *blood* in the name is out."

"Good call, because it's also known as stink bait."

Ewww… "Definitely bass."

"Bass it is. Now move to the edge of the boat."

After she complied, Paris surveyed the wooded bank and noticed not a house, or soul, in sight. "How many people live on this lake?"

"Just me and George," he said. "It's a private lake."

Of course it was. "So there's no chance anyone will see me making a fool of myself?"

"Not likely." Dallas came up behind her and handed her the pole with the little yellow frog-looking thingy dangling from the end. "Hold this in your left hand, and grasp the reel in your right."

Simple enough. "Like this?"

"Yep. Now push that button with your thumb, pull the rod back to the side and let it go, but not over your head or you'll hook me."

She did exactly as he'd instructed, yet nothing happened. "I knew I wasn't cut out for this."

"I don't mind helping you out." He moved behind her, wrapped his hand around the rod below her hand and replaced her thumb on the release with his. "It's just one smooth action," he said as he cast the line in the water with ease.

He didn't make a move away from her. In fact, Paris would swear he moved closer. "Okay. What now?"

He rested a palm on her belly and pushed her hair to one side with the other. "It's a top-water jig, so the fish will hit it on top of the water."

"How long does that take?"

"Until the fish decides to bite."

When Dallas rimmed the shell of her ear with his tongue, Paris almost dropped the pole. "So it might take a while."

"Probably not."

After Dallas dropped his arms from around her, Paris glanced back to find he'd removed his shirt. And oh, what a sight to behold. He had a board-flat belly and a chest that wouldn't quit. "Hot already?"

"Lady, you have no idea how hot."

She had a sneaking suspicion she might soon find out when he came back to her and began kissing her neck again. "What are you up to, Dallas Calloway?"

He moved flush against her back. "Pay me no mind and watch your line, in case you get a bite."

"Aren't you going to fish?"

"Maybe later. I have something I'd rather do at the moment."

Paris held her breath when he tugged the string at her neck and unclasped the strap at her back. Now the bikini top lay in a pool at her feet and she found herself exactly where she'd been last night—naked from the waist up.

"Dallas, are you sure no one will see us?" Her voice sounded tinny, thanks to the cowboy's hands roving over her breasts.

"George left for Kerrville this morning to visit his mother." He feathered more kisses along her neck. "Besides, the possibility of getting caught makes this a little more exciting."

Her legs began to shake like a leaf in the breeze. "Any more excitement and I might actually not be able to stand."

"I'll make sure you don't fall. Just relax."

Relaxing proved to be impossible when his palm came to rest on her midriff and began to drift lower… and lower. "What are you doing now?"

"Scratching your itch."

When he slipped his hand beneath her bathing suit bottoms, Paris was powerless to stop him. When he began to stroke her softly, she could no longer hold onto the fishing pole. After she dropped it on the deck, she reached back and wrapped her hand around his nape to ground herself. She briefly envisioned how this would look to a passerby—him with his hand down her pants and her in the throes of a sexual frenzy—and that only amplified her need for release.

In a matter of seconds, her pulse accelerated and her respiration picked up speed as the impending climax began to build. The orgasm slammed into her hard with a series of strong spasms that seemed as if they went on forever. She literally shook from the force of it and Dallas, as if he sensed she might not remain upright, turned her into his arms and kissed her.

She came back to reality slowly and broke the kiss to tip her forehead against his shoulder. "Wow."

"Been a while, has it?"

"Try never. At least not with Peter."

He set her back and stared at her. "He never got you off?"

She shook her head. "Sadly no, because he really didn't try, or care. And go ahead and say it. I'm a fool for staying with him as long as I did."

His expression turned somber. "Then why did you?"

"Because I'd convinced myself I couldn't do any better." An admission she'd not made to herself, much less to another soul.

He hugged her for a few moments then pulled away to study her eyes. "Sweetheart, you deserve better. You deserve to have a lover who takes care of you first and puts himself second. That's the way a man should treat his woman, especially a woman as special as you."

His woman? Once upon a time she would have made a snide comment about beating his chest, but oddly she liked the sound of it. "Thank you. That means more than you know. But I'm nothing special."

He looked mock serious. "Yes, you are, and don't argue with me."

"I wouldn't dare, Mr. Macho. Not after what you just did for me." That brought about an important question. "Speaking of that, what about you? You've clearly got an itch that needs scratching, too."

"True, but I'm fine for now." He grinned. "Later this evening is another story altogether. We still have a whole lot of exploring to do, if you're game."

Paris imagined giving him the pleasure he'd just given her and that made her tingle. "I'm definitely game." The sound of the reel suddenly drew her attention and prompted her to snatch the rod off the ground. "I think I have something. What do I do now?"

"Bring it in, darlin'."

"How?"

Without responding, Dallas stepped to her side, took the pole and turned the reel's handle until he brought up the line, a smallish silver fish dangling from the hook. "Not quite big enough for dinner."

"It's so cute, but hurry and take it off."

"It's a baby," he said as he unhooked the bass, crouched down and released it into the water. "Grow up, bud, and maybe I'll catch ya later."

That made Paris smile. "I'm glad you let him go."

"I don't like fishermen who hang on to undersized fish just because they can. It's a waste, and I don't like waste."

She liked him more and more with each passing moment. She predicted that beneath the tough-guy exterior resided a heart of gold. "It's nice to know you have respect for wildlife. And women."

He offered her the pole. "Want to try for something bigger?"

"Are you referring to a fish?" she teased.

"Well, sweetheart, what else do you have in mind?"

"Maybe I'll show you later this evening." She took the rod and this time managed to cast it all by herself. "How was that?"

"Looks like you're a fast learner."

She handed him back the pole. "But I'm not very patient. You fish, I'll just kick back on the deck, get some sun and watch you bring in dinner."

He nodded toward the hatch. "There's a towel in there, so have fun. But don't get too comfortable because we might not be here much longer. It's almost time for lunch."

Paris realized she hadn't eaten a thing since the whole grain bar she'd consumed in the bedroom following her novice strip tease. "I admit I'm getting a little hungry, too."

After casting toward the bank, Dallas shot her a grin. "From this point forward, you can always depend on me to take care of all your appetites. How am I doing so far?"

She returned his smile. "Best fishing trip ever."

And she couldn't wait to find out what else he had planned.

Seven

His plans for Paris had unfortunately been put on hold.

The woman had been so relaxed that immediately after she'd eaten lunch—if you wanted to call a tomato and lettuce sandwich *lunch*—she'd taken a nap. A long nap.

His mind whirled back to earlier in the day, when she'd been as hot as a branding iron and quick to fire. The bastard she'd married had done a number on her, and he really wanted to right the wrongs. Show her all the ways a man could please a woman. Convince her that she was as close to perfect as they come. No doubt he'd be up for the challenge, in every way possible.

Dallas had thought about joining her in bed, but he'd taken a trip to the nearest grocery store—fifteen miles away—then returned a few calls, including one from his attorney. As a result of that conversation, he had to break some serious news that wouldn't make Paris happy in the least. She might not want anything more to do with him.

And now, with the sun working its way down the horizon, Dallas grabbed a beer, fired up the grill and contemplated how he would tell her the sorry news. He didn't have a lot of time left, he realized, when Paris made an appearance on the back deck a few minutes later, looking like she'd walked right off the cover of a fashion magazine.

Her straight blond hair fell past her shoulders like homespun silk. She wore just enough makeup to show off her features to full advantage, and a short blue dress with thin straps that showed enough cleavage to make him want to growl. He couldn't believe his luck in finding such a good-looking fake wife.

She kicked off her flip-flops, curled up on the wicker sofa and pulled her legs beneath her on the blue cushions. "Whatcha doing, cowboy?"

Imagining what it would be like to make fast, hard love to you on that sofa. For the sake of distraction, Dallas turned the burgers before lowering the lid on the grill to regard her again. "I'm making us some dinner. You must've been really tired considering how long you slept."

"I only slept about an hour. I spent the rest of the time rehearsing what I would tell my parents about our marriage and then I called them."

He would have liked to have been a fly on the wall during that conversation. "How did it go?"

She shrugged. "As expected. My mom bemoaned the fact that once again she didn't have the opportunity to throw a lavish wedding for her youngest daughter due to a whirlwind courtship. The conversation with my dad wasn't much better."

"What did he say?"

"He said, and I quote, 'This guy better not treat you as poorly as that other SOB.' And then he went on to say to let him know where he can find Peter so he can beat the…well…some sense into him."

Although Dallas could understand her father's attitude toward the ex-husband, he didn't like the thought of winding up on the wrong side of a retired military man when that man learned his daughter's latest marriage wasn't permanent. "How big is your dad?"

"How tall are you?"

"Six-two."

"He's five inches shorter and stocky. My mom is five-seven, and so is my sister. I fell on the shorter side at five-five."

"I would've guessed you to be a little bit taller. Must be those long legs."

"Must be your imagination."

Yeah, his imagination was running amok when he thought about having those legs wrapped around his waist. Again he looked to his cooking duty to keep him from acting on his fantasies. At least until he could confess…after dinner.

"Speaking of family dynamics," Paris began, "I assume all your brothers know about the will, but do they know that our marriage isn't exactly the real thing?"

"They're all pretty busy right now so I'm not sure what Jen or Maria have told them. I plan to say as little as possible when we get back to the ranch."

"Do you think they would actually believe you would rush into a marriage on a whim because of a will?"

Probably not. "It doesn't matter what they believe. It's an unspoken rule that we don't get into each other's business."

After a span of silence, Paris leaned slightly and studied the grill. "Color me crazy, Dallas, but those look a lot like beef patties."

"Only two of them," he said as he flipped them again before turning back to Paris. "I found some kind of veggie burgers at the store. I figured they couldn't be too bad. Heck, you could serve up a boot as long as you've grilled it with mesquite wood chips."

"Heavens, I hope it doesn't taste like a boot."

Honestly, so did Dallas. He didn't want to let her down, although he suspected he eventually would before night's end. "The cashier who checked me out told me she loved them."

"I'll bet she checked you out thoroughly."

The jealously in her voice surprised him, and in some ways pleased him. "She had to be at least sixty-five."

She lifted her chin. "Just because a woman matures doesn't mean she can't recognize a sexy cowboy when she sees one."

"And just because I'm a man doesn't mean I'm gonna flirt with a grandmother."

"Men flirt with any woman who'll flirt back."

At least she'd said it with a smile. She wouldn't be

smiling when he lowered the legal boom. "Do you want something to drink?"

"I wouldn't turn down a glass of white wine, if you happen to have some. If not, water will work."

"I have wine." Thankfully he'd had the foresight to stock up a few months ago, the last time he'd had a female guest at the cabin. The last time he'd had a woman, period. Tina, or maybe it was Terry. What the hell did it matter? He'd only spent one weekend with her. Plus, she couldn't hold a candle to Paris in any way, shape or form.

When Paris came to her feet, Dallas caught a good glimpse of a thigh and one stubborn part of him stood, too. He needed to get the hell out of Dodge before she noticed. He'd begun to wonder if any man had ever expired due to a perpetual erection. "Sit. I'll bring it to you. In the meantime, you enjoy the sunset."

"If you leave, you'll miss it since it's almost gone."

So was his sanity. "I've seen it before." He'd also seen a feminine leg before, but for some reason, viewing even an inch of her bare skin kicked his libido into overdrive.

After one last look at the burgers, Dallas rushed into the house, braced both palms on the kitchen island and took a few deep breaths. If he didn't calm down and get with the program, all his plans for the evening would go up in smoke. He couldn't act on his need for her until she knew all the truth.

When he finally gained his composure, he took the plate full of lettuce, tomatoes and pickles from the fridge, along with the bottle of chardonnay. He thought about popping the top on another beer but figured that wouldn't help his predicament at all. He needed to keep his guard up and his sex drive down for the time being.

He brought the hamburger fixings and put them on the wooden picnic table, then handed Paris the wine. "Sorry about the plastic cup. I don't have any fancy barware here. Hell, I don't have any fancy dinnerware, either. That's why we're eating on disposable plates."

She took a drink of the chardonnay and rested the cup in her lap. "Not exactly environmentally friendly, but I suppose they'll do if we don't have a choice."

He didn't want her to believe he was a total Neanderthal. "They're plastic, too. I throw them in the recycle bin before I leave so George can properly dispose of them."

"That's good to know. How is dinner coming along?"

He checked the burgers, all the while considering giving her a kiss. Only one kiss. But like the potato chips resting on the red checkerboard tablecloth, he wouldn't be able to stop with just one. "Looks like they're about ready. Do you want cheese on yours?"

"Sure. I'm in the mood to splurge a little."

Dallas hadn't realized she was standing behind him until that moment. After laying the cheese slices on the burgers, he put the spatula down and turned around, only to run headlong into some fairly fantastic green eyes and a mouth that looked like it wanted to be kissed. Maybe that was just wishful thinking. "What else are you in the mood for?"

She slid her arms around his neck and pressed her great body against his, indicating she might be willing to make his wish come true. "Oh, I don't know. Maybe a little slap and tickle after we eat. Maybe a little of that before we eat."

Man, she was killing him. "Aren't you hungry?"

"Yes, but not only for food." She rubbed against him and it hadn't been an accident. "Just humor me, okay?"

With the last scrap of his control in shambles, Dallas gave her a full-throttle, no-holds-barred kiss. A tongue-dueling, fire-starting kiss that gave the barbecue grill behind him a run for its money.

But damn, he wanted more. He wanted to use his mouth somewhere else, and that meant disregarding his original plan of ignoring her. To hell with it.

He pushed the straps off her shoulders and then lowered the dress's bodice to do what he'd wanted to do earlier that day. He bent his head and took one breast into his mouth while Paris threaded her hands through his hair to hang on. When he circled her nipple with his tongue, she released a purely sexual sound that made him so hard he wanted to strip out of his jeans then and there. Instead, he slid his palms down her back, clasped her butt and pulled her against the erection that wouldn't die unless he did something about it. But if he acted in haste, he could make a mistake of monumental proportions. As bad as he wanted to be inside her, he thought of all the reasons why he couldn't.

Dallas let her go and took a step back. He had to look her straight in the eye when he made the revelation. "We need to have a serious talk before this goes any further."

Paris's lips looked swollen and her eyes hazy, but she

didn't seem to be too mad over the interruption. Yet. "Talk about what?"

"A change in the marriage terms."

"I'm sorry, Dallas, but I'm confused."

She wouldn't be confused much longer, but she sure as hell might be ready to slug him. He saw no choice but to blurt out the sorry truth.

"Darlin', we're going to have to get divorced."

Surely she hadn't heard him correctly. "Are you serious?"

"Yeah, I am."

Paris pulled the dress back into place as her mind reeled from Dallas's proclamation. "Now? We've barely been married a day."

"No, not now. When the year ends."

She could not believe he would go back on his word. So much for trusting another man. "We both agreed we would get an annulment. In fact, you promised your attorney would find some way to accomplish that goal."

Dallas took her by the hand and showed her to the table where they sat on opposing benches. "I spoke to him today," he began, "to ask him why it was taking so long to get the final agreement drawn up. He informed me that if we annul the marriage, that would be like it never existed in the first place, and that would go against the terms of the will."

Darn the family feud. She struggled to remain calm and sensible when she wanted to shout from frustration. "Then Worth could take control of the ranch and this charade would have been for naught."

"That about sums it up."

And she didn't like it one iota. "Great. We'll be forced to get a divorce and I'll be marked as a woman who just can't make any marriage work."

"Not if the divorce is my fault and I take the fall."

She supposed at this point they didn't have any choice. "How would you do that?"

"You could tell everyone I cheated on you."

Impossible. "That would be two cheating husbands. People could interpret that as I'm a total fool, or a cold fish in bed. What else do you have?"

"Maybe I drink too much."

She'd never seen him have more than one beer. "Anyone who knows you could disprove that. Any other brilliant ideas?"

"Yeah, I could tell the truth. I don't want any kids and that's a deal breaker for you."

Shock rendered her momentarily silent. Under the circumstances, that shouldn't matter to her, but it did. His disclosure did put the kibosh on any future with him, as if she'd really believed that would happen. "You don't want a child to continue your legacy?"

"Nope. I have five brothers who can take care of the procreating."

For a man who appeared to be all about family, he certainly seemed opposed to having one of his own. "Why exactly do you feel this way?"

He stared at some unknown focal point behind her. "When you have the misfortune of being born to a man like my dad, it makes you doubt yourself and your ability to be a good husband and father."

She reached over and touched his hand to garner his attention. "As far as I know, infidelity isn't genetic, and I sense you'd be a great father."

"You don't know me that well."

True, but she believed she was getting there. And she still had twelve months to learn even more, although she realized that was all she would ever have with him. "I know you love animals and you're willing to set a baby bass free. That speaks to your patience and compassion and some paternal instinct."

"I'm basically married to someone for the sake of a parcel of land. Some might say that speaks to my selfishness."

Obviously both of them put a lot of stock in other people's opinions. "I don't see you as selfish, just desperate. Besides, I'm basically in the same situation since I married for financial stability. Mr. and Mrs. Desperation. It has a nice ring to it."

He rubbed his chin then grinned. "Yeah, it does. So you're not too mad at me over the annulment issue?"

She wanted to be angry, but in essence she could only blame faulty research and jumping in feet first before they knew all the facts. "Let's just say I'm disappointed we rushed into this before I fully investigated our options"

"Would you have changed your mind if you'd known?"

She had to think about that a few seconds. "Possibly, but it doesn't matter since we can't do anything about it now. Besides, we still have twelve months to figure out how we're going to end it."

"Yeah, you're right, unless you can't tolerate me that long."

She gave him a mock stern look. "That's a strong possibility if you don't finish those burgers. I'm suddenly so hungry I could eat the tablecloth."

"No more slap and tickle?" he asked, clear disappointment in his tone.

She wanted to say definitely, but she hadn't quite digested the divorce issue. "Let's worry about dinner right now, okay?"

He stood and leaned over to kiss her forehead. "Sure thing, sweetheart."

Something suddenly occurred to her. "Since it is your birthday, I should have cooked for you."

He studied her a long moment before speaking again. "You know what I'd really like from you to make this day special?"

"Does it start with an 's' and rhyme with vex?"

He shook his head. "No. I want you to tell me you believe that I didn't know the annulment wasn't going to work."

"I'm going to give you the benefit of the doubt." And she hoped her faith wasn't misplaced again. "I only wish we'd had more time to think things through before we rushed into this arrangement."

"Unfortunately time wasn't on our side. But I'll try to make it up to you after dinner."

That could create more problems from an emotional standpoint if she succumbed to her strong desire for him. "How are you going to do that?"

"You'll have to wait and see."

* * *

The sound of a sultry country ballad drew Paris from the kitchen back onto the deck. As the music filtered through the outdoor speakers, the sun had disappeared from the horizon, washing the sky in an orange glow, providing the perfect backdrop to the man leaning back against the railing. A cowboy knight wearing a crisp light blue shirt rolled up at the sleeves, slightly faded jeans and the usual boots, one substantial hand wrapped around a beer.

"Did you shower?" she asked as she approached Dallas, immediately catching a whiff of his clean-scented cologne.

"I wanted to get rid of the barbecue smells."

"I really don't mind that at all." And she didn't, though she still worried she'd made a mistake with their fake marriage. She worried she might make another if she didn't keep her wits about her.

"Thanks for cleaning up the mess," he said.

"After those great veggie burgers, it was the least I could do."

A few moments of silence ticked off as they stood there steeped in palpable tension. Dallas shifted his weight from one leg to the other before setting the bottle atop the nearby table. "Let's dance," he said as he offered his hand to her.

Paris was plagued with a serious case of nerves. "I'm not very good. Not when it comes to country dancing."

He pulled her gently into his arms. "You just have to hold on to me."

And she did as they swayed in time to the tune, moving easily through the last of the song and onto the next, his palms roving softly over her back, her cheek resting against his shoulder.

She briefly wondered how many women had fallen under his spell. How many would have given anything to be in her shoes right now. That shouldn't matter. After all, they were married, at least for a year until it all came to an end.

Maybe they could take the time to learn more about each other. Perhaps she should spend the months finding herself, without getting lost in him. But she felt lost right then as they moved closer, held each other tighter.

When Dallas paused, Paris lifted her head and met his mesmerizing blue eyes. "Mind if I kiss you?" he asked.

She found that odd. "You've never needed my permission before."

"Yeah, but I do now since I didn't keep my promise to you about the annulment."

"It's done, Dallas. We can't go back and undo it. We can only move forward."

"True. You didn't answer my question."

She did, but not with words, despite the lack of wisdom. Instead, she wrapped her hands around his neck and kissed him. A soft, almost quiet kiss that seemed strangely emotional. The way newlyweds who had entered a real union would kiss. A kiss that took a drastic turn toward mutual need in a matter of moments.

Dallas broke the contact first and sighed. "I wish I didn't want you so damn bad."

In some ways she wished the same for herself. But

life was short, and their time limited. She could reject his advances, or take another risk that would most definitely come with rewards. Foolish as it might be, she wanted to experience all that he had to offer, and suffer the possible consequences later. "Maybe we shouldn't overthink this too much."

He frowned. "I'm not following you."

"Do you know what this divorce requirement means?"

"Yeah. I'm going to be padding my lawyer's pockets even more."

Evidently he was having a lapse in comprehension. "No. What it means for us."

He grinned. "We don't have to stop with only slappin' and ticklin'?"

She did a little smiling, too. "Correct."

His smile faded into a serious expression. "That's a big step, Paris."

A step she hadn't planned to take, but… "As you've said, we're both consenting adults and we'll be spending a lot of time together. Since the consummation issue no longer exists, we have no reason not to let nature take its course." And during the journey, she vowed to keep a good grip on her heart.

Taking her by the hand, he led her back to the table, claimed the bench across from her, folded his hands and gave her a somber look. "Are you sure you want to do this? I don't want you to feel like you're being pressured into something that makes you uncomfortable."

Evidently he didn't get it. "Let me put it to you this way. For the first thirty years of my life, I walked a straight line. I ignorantly thought if I followed all the rules, did what was expected, didn't make waves, everything would be rosy. I learned a painful lesson when I realized that wasn't always the case two years ago."

"After your divorce?"

She wanted so badly to tell him the whole truth, but only one person could verify that, and Peter wasn't talking. "The divorce turned out to be only the beginning. Once I lost my job, I recognized that no matter how well you walk the line, situations arise that steer you off your path. I determined then and there I would make my own decisions and guide my own future. As ridiculous as it seems, this agreement we made happened to be a step in the right direction. Otherwise, I would not have entered into it."

He frowned. "You still haven't answered my concerns."

"Actually, yes I have. If I want to be carefree and enjoy intimacy with my pseudohusband, then I'm going to do it. More importantly, I trust you, Dallas. I know you're going to treat me well and make me feel respected. So there."

He finally sent her that wonderful smile again. "Okay then. You've convinced me you're ready."

She wondered if maybe he was experiencing a little hesitation. "Are you ready?"

"Darlin' that is not a question you should have to ask."

Paris felt a disclaimer coming on. "We can do this as long as we go inside and turn off the lights since I assume I'm going to be completely naked."

He stood, rounded the table and held out his hand to help her up. "Inside is okay and we're both going to be naked. Besides, I've already seen a lot of your body, and I want to see it all, so I won't promise I'll turn off lights."

"Dallas—"

He cut off her protest with a quick kiss. "If you really trust me, then let me show you the benefits of seeing all the details."

Exactly what she wanted to avoid. But maybe the time had come to shed her self-consciousness in earnest. Maybe she could actually take charge of the situation and finally relax.

Mulling that over, Paris followed Dallas inside, expecting to be led into the bedroom. Instead, he went to the opposite end of the house and past the kitchen to an all-glass sun porch with rustic, wide, cushioned chaises and plush, rug-covered slate floors. Through the wall of windows, she glimpsed a small creek and two deer foraging in the grassy area in the last remnants of daylight. "Why have I never seen this place?"

"Because you haven't been here long enough to explore," he said. "During the day, you get sun. At night, you can see all the stars. If you notice, there aren't any light fixtures."

She looked around to confirm that fact. She also noted the room was illuminated enough to view all those details she preferred he not see. "Is this where you bring all your dates?"

He didn't appear too pleased over the question. "This is where I come to wind down."

"It's a good place to do it. Unwind, I mean."

He cupped her cheek with his palm. "It's a good place for us to get to know each other in every way."

They stood there face-to-face, as if neither knew what to do next. Dallas broke the standoff by taking her back into his arms and holding her for a long moment. He pulled away and searched her eyes. "If you change your mind at any point, let me know. I want you to be totally comfortable."

She very much appreciated his consideration. She also felt confident he would show her great care, and probably a very good time. "I'm not going to change my mind."

He sent her a soft smile. "Good. I've been waiting all night to see you undress for me."

Oh, mercy. "Are you going to watch?"

He flashed a grin and a dimple. "Do politicians lie?"

"All right. I suppose I can do that. As you pointed out, you've seen almost all of me anyway." And now he would see it all—from head to toe and too-wide hips in between.

You're too uptight, Paris.

The ghost of that chunky, awkward girl came back to haunt her, along with the voice of her ex criticizing her butt and in his opinion, inadequate breasts. She lowered her eyes to avoid Dallas's scrutiny. "I'm not sure I can do this while you're staring at me."

He came to her then, tipped up her chin with his fingertips and kissed her softly. "Yeah, you can. Don't forget the boat."

"That was different. I had on a bikini until you took the top off me. And that was only the top."

She could tell by his expression that his patience was waning. "You're a beautiful woman, Paris. All of you. Now we can talk about this all night, or we can act on this all-fire need between us."

"Okay, I admit there is a tad bit of chemistry."

"You know we've both been hot for each other since we met. You can keep denying it, but you know I'm right. I figured that out in the kitchen this morning when you dropped the robe. If that wasn't a hint, then I don't know what is."

She couldn't be shocked when she'd intentionally been transparent. She'd also allowed him a peek of her backside, and he hadn't run away yet. "Okay, I'll make a deal with you. Since you've already seen more of me than I care to admit, it's only fair you go first."

Without hesitating, he stepped back and lowered his fly. "Just so you know, something's come up. It's been up for days."

She managed a smile. "Nothing I haven't seen before."

After stripping out of his clothes and underwear, he looked no less proud. Every inch of him. And frankly, her very limited sexual experience had not included such an absolutely impressive…man.

"It's your turn, sweetheart."

Okay, she could do this. She'd been pretty gutsy this morning. Why not carry that over to this moment?

Following a deep breath, Paris shimmied out of the dress and let it fall to her feet, then shoved her panties down and kicked them aside. And there she stood, totally nude in the middle of a dimly-lit, glass-walled room with a fantasy man raking his gaze over her, clear approval in his eyes.

He inclined his head and pointed at her. "Lady, if I had my choice, you'd never wear a thing again when you're with me."

She released an anxious laugh. "Something tells me that could be awkward with both the mothers darting in and out all the time."

"True. Now come here and let me give you the time of your life."

Paris felt much less ill at ease and very ready to be in his arms. "Gladly."

Dallas grabbed a pillow from one chaise, set it down on the largest rug, then signaled her to join him on the floor. He laid her back and hovered above her a few moments as he stroked her cheek. They kissed for a long while as if they didn't have a worry in the world. She did find it strange that he hadn't exactly ravished her, and very curious when he said, "I need to get something."

When Dallas left her embrace, Paris felt bereft. "Hope you hurry back."

"Darlin', you won't even know I'm gone."

Perhaps he wasn't quite that quick, but he did return in less than two minutes, carrying that "something" in his hand. She sat up and braced on bent arms. "Just so you know, I am on the pill."

"Doesn't matter," he said as he stretched out next to her on his side. "No birth control is fail proof so having both is better. Nothing wrong with a double bucket, as we say in the horse world."

The seriousness in his tone told Paris he truly didn't want a child, and she found that sad. However, getting pregnant in this situation would be completely inadvisable and cause for great concern. "I totally agree with using both. Besides, in this day and time, safety should also come into play."

"I'm safe, just don't want to be sorry."

After Dallas tossed the condom aside, he kissed his way down her throat, pausing to pay special attention to her breasts, barring all thoughts or concerns from her brain. But he didn't linger very long before sending his talented mouth down her torso, lower and lower, causing Paris to shift with anticipation.

He lifted his head and rested his chin on her belly. "Are you okay?"

Apparently he'd misinterpreted her movement. "Never better."

"Just wanted to be sure this is something you want."

"It's something I've never had before." Only one more admission that pointed to the sad state of her sex life and the severe lack of intimacy with her former husband.

Her current husband, on the other hand, looked as if she'd awarded him the grand prize for being such a gracious lover. "I will almost guarantee you're going to like it. But if not, let me know."

When Dallas's mouth hit home between her trembling legs, Paris couldn't speak if her life depended it. She could barely even breathe. She couldn't manage to keep her eyes open, though. Every featherlight stroke of his tongue brought her closer to the brink of madness. Every pull of his lips drove her further into oblivion, but not enough to tune out the steady build of the climax as he lifted her hips with his palms, bringing her closer to his expert mouth. And then came the strongest, mind-blowing climax she'd ever experienced.

She almost screamed but somehow quelled it. She couldn't stop the slight moan that drifted from her mouth or the inadvert movement of her hips. She did miss the moment Dallas rose up, she realized, when her eyes fluttered open to discover him tearing at the silver package with his teeth.

He seemed to be quite in a hurry and that might have made her smile except she wanted him to hurry, too. He also seemed to be a pro when he had the condom in place in a matter of seconds.

Paris refused to think about his past conquests. She wanted only to concentrate on all the sensations as Dallas shifted over and eased inside. She rubbed her palms over his muscled back as he moved in a slow, delicious rhythm. She circled her legs around his waist, allowing him to go deeper with each thrust. He demonstrated his stamina, his control, as they continued this dance she'd been determined to avoid. And when that control slipped, his body tensed and he collapsed against her with a low groan.

Paris truly cherished the feel of his weight, the feel of this man who'd entered her life and turned her world upside down. She honestly mourned the loss of him when he rolled onto his back and draped one arm over his eyes.

"That happened way too fast," he said.

She shifted to her side and studied him a few minutes. "Out of ten, I'd give that a twelve."

"A twenty," he muttered. "You're definitely a natural."

"And you're definitely an expert."

He turned to face her. "Don't ever doubt that you're special, sweetheart."

Funny, he made her feel that way. "I must admit I did surprise myself."

He could move mountains with that grin. "I'm ready for another round. How about you?"

"Maybe we could do it under the table outside since we have yet to explore that scenario. Heck, maybe we could do it *on* the table."

He narrowed his eyes and tried to look disapproving. "Have I turned my good girl bad?"

My good girl... If only that were true. "You know, I think you have."

"I'm glad. I wouldn't want you any other way."

She wished he wanted her for all time.

The sudden thought took Paris by storm. She had to emotionally stand firm and avoid any fuzzy feelings if she wanted to protect herself. Yet when Dallas held her again, she worried she might travel straight into the land of heartache.

Eight

During the past week, his good girl turned bad had pretty much worn him out. Not at all a complaint, just an accurate observation. But as soon as they returned to the ranch today, Dallas had to resume his usual routine.

He'd let a lot of things slide, including joining Tyler to search for prime rodeo stock for Texas Extreme. But as he felt his wife's hand beneath the sheet, he didn't give a damn about duty. He had to have her. Now.

They came together in a rush of kisses, a hot, quick roll. A morning drive-by, as Paris had put it. He knew exactly how to touch her to give her what she needed. She knew exactly how to move to send him over the edge. By the time they were done, they were both pretty much exhausted.

Dallas rolled onto his back and studied the ceiling,

waiting for his breathing to calm and his heart to slow down. "You're incredible, darlin'."

"You're not so bad yourself, cowboy." She draped her arm across his belly. "I wish we could stay here a little longer."

He stacked his hands behind his head and sighed. "I didn't intend to be here this long, but a pretty little lady decided to hold me hostage."

She playfully slapped at his arm. "I didn't hold you hostage, Dallas. You were free to go at any point in time."

"Let me rephrase that. You made me a prisoner with your good loving."

She remained quiet for a moment before asking, "What's going to happen after we're back at the ranch?"

"Business as usual."

"I meant with us. Do I sleep in the guest room or in your room?"

He hadn't given that much thought, but he didn't like not having her in his bed. "We should probably give the appearance of the happily married newlyweds."

She laid her head on his shoulder and sighed. "Honestly, I can't remember the last time I've been this happy. It's been a wonderful week."

Uh-oh. If she got stars in her eyes, that could spell trouble. "It's been great, but it's not reality. You and I both know this arrangement comes to an end in a year."

She rose up and stared at him. "You don't have to remind me of that. But if I'm going to be stuck in this pretense, I don't see any reason why we can't enjoy each other's company, unless you decide that once we leave here, the party's over."

He saw a major reason why they shouldn't enjoy it too much. "I still want to be with you, just as long as you know I'm not looking for anything permanent."

The comment sent her out of the bed to grab her robe and slide it on before she faced him. "Of course it's not permanent, Dallas. If I learned anything about you at all since we met, it's that for some reason you run from emotional commitment."

That made him sound like a coward. "Look, I'm not running from anything. I just know who I am, darlin', and if you expect too much, I'll break your heart."

She tightened the sash and pushed her hair away from her face. "Don't flatter yourself. I'm much tougher than you think."

Spinning around, Paris headed into the bathroom and shut the door a little harder than necessary. Dallas remained in the same spot, pondering her words. Maybe in some ways she'd been right. Maybe he had been running away. But one thing he'd learned in life—aside from most of his immediate family, people never stayed around for very long, if not physically, then emotionally. He recalled the loneliness following his mother's death. He'd witnessed both Maria's and Jen's devastation when they'd learned of his dad's betrayal. He wasn't going to put himself out there to be hung up to dry.

He'd been a loner much of his life, and he liked it that way. Even a special woman like Paris couldn't change his mind.

* * *

Little by little, everything had begun to change over the past few days. Even though Paris had opted to stay in his suite, he hadn't touched her. She'd gone to bed before him, and he'd started getting up before her. No more predawn lovemaking. No more joking around. In fact, he'd barely spoken to her aside from general conversation over meals. When she'd asked Dallas if something was wrong, he'd only said he'd been busy playing catch-up. It seemed as if everything they'd shared at the cabin had all been a dream. Today she planned to get to the bottom of his sudden turnaround.

After a futile search for him in the barn, Paris hopped into her new black luxury sedan—a wedding gift from her new husband—then drove to the main office and marched in, bent on seeking him out. "Is Dallas here?"

Jenny patted her big hair and smiled. "No, sugar, he's not here. He left for the house about a half hour ago. I believe he's in the media room."

Oh, for heavens sake. She should have checked there first. "Are you sure?"

"That's what he told me when I put your dinner in the oven. I made a nice vegetarian lasagna. It should be ready in ten minutes or so and you'll find a salad in the fridge."

Eating alone didn't exactly appeal to her. "Thanks, but I need to talk to Dallas before I even think about dinner."

Jenny took on a concerned look. "Is something wrong, sugar?"

"No." She reconsidered when she realized the stepmom could be a solid sounding board. "Actually, yes. Since we returned from the cabin, he's been rather aloof."

"Oh, that. I'm not surprised."

Clearly everyone else in the Calloway family held the key to Dallas's mood. "Could you let me in on the secret?"

"I will gladly fill you in, since my stepson isn't one to talk about his feelings."

Paris knew that all too well. "Go ahead. I'm all ears."

"First of all, his mother died on April second, which happens to be tomorrow. Coincidentally, J.D. died April third. According to Maria, and I've seen it myself since I've been here, Dallas goes into this funk. Give him a week or so and he'll come back around."

Most of that made sense, but she believed there could be more. She also found it hard to believe he would do a one-eighty when it came to their floundering personal relationship. "Maybe it's time someone encourages him to get in touch with his feelings."

"Be careful, Paris," Jenny cautioned. "If you push too hard, he'll only withdraw more."

Not if she could help it. "I'll approach the issue slowly. Thanks for telling me."

"You're welcome, sugar, and good luck. By the way, you never said if you enjoyed your honeymoon."

She had been intentionally guarded in what she'd revealed for fear Jenny would read too much into it. Regardless, the honeymoon phase was basically over before it had really begun. "We had a very nice time. I'll see you later."

Paris rushed out of the office before Jenny began requesting details. After she made it back to the house, she hurried up the stairs and headed to the cowboy cave, only to find the door closed. She considered knocking but since he might not answer, she decided to walk right in.

Dallas looked surprised to see her, but she happened to be more surprised to see him seated at a round table, a slew of photographs spread out before him.

"I thought I might find you here," she said as she pulled out a chair. "What are those, if you don't mind me asking?"

He slid a picture of a brown-haired, blue-eyed young woman holding a toddler, a black horse grazing beside them. "That's my mom, Carol."

The first time she'd heard him mention his mother's name. "And you?"

"Yeah and her mare, Kenya."

"She's beautiful. Your mom, not the horse, although the horse is pretty, too. You definitely have her eyes. Your mom's eyes, not the horse."

Finally she'd unearthed his smile but it faded fast. "That's the horse that killed her."

Paris swallowed around her shock. "How did that happen?"

He leaned back in the chair and streaked a hand over his jaw. "She was training her for speed events. Kenya spooked one day and threw her into a barrel. She sustained a serious head injury and died two days later."

The pain in his voice was palpable. "Do you remember any of that?"

"No. I just recall she was there one day and not the next. I didn't find out what happened until I asked my dad when I turned thirteen. Of course, he didn't want to talk about it so Maria told me."

Thank heavens he'd been spared the details when he'd been too young to understand. She leaned over and picked up a photo of a twentysomething, tall, handsome man with a single prominent dimple. The resemblance to Dallas was almost uncanny. "I assume this is your father."

"The one and only. That was taken right after he married Maria."

She'd always wanted to know how that had come about, and now she had her chance. "When and how did they meet?"

"He hired her as our nanny after my mom died. Next thing I knew, they married a few months later. Then came Houston and Tyler."

"No doubt about it, your dad didn't waste any time."

"No. He just wasted the truth."

Paris wished he could find a way to heal, and she could find a way to help. "Don't waste your life being bitter, Dallas. I had to tell myself if I let my anger toward Peter continue to rule my life, I would lose and he would win."

He nailed her with a stern look. "Maybe I'm not the eternal optimist, like you."

"Then it seems to me you're very much like Fort."

He mulled that over for a moment, as if he'd never considered that notion, before the ire returned. "I'm nothing like him. I didn't abandon the entire family due to the sins of the father."

She might as well beat her forehead against the table. "No, but you might be abandoning your happiness by keeping yourself closed off to it. And shutting me out isn't going to make me go away, if that's what you're thinking."

He failed to look at her. "I'm not shutting you out."

"Oh, really? I don't remember the last time you kissed me, much less touched me. I wake up in the middle of the night and you're on the edge of the bed as if you can't stand to be near me. If you find it so appalling to sleep with me, just let me know. I'll be glad to move to a guest room."

"I don't find you appalling, dammit. It's just that—"

"What?"

"I never wanted to hurt you, Paris, but it sure looks like I'm doing that now. I'm worried maybe you have expectations I can't meet."

Feeling a bit more benevolent, she laid a palm on his arm. "You can't hurt me unless I allow it, and I'm not going to do that. And I don't expect anything from you that you can't give. I'm a big girl and I know what I agreed to when I married you. But I would like better communication between us."

"I'm not real good at that and I'm not sure I can change."

With a retort on the tip of her tongue, Paris suddenly remembered she hadn't removed the food from the oven. "Dinner should be ready by now. We can continue this conversation while we eat."

"I'm not hungry," he said. "You go ahead. I'll grab something later."

Paris's frustration began to mount. "I don't deserve this, Dallas."

He shuffled through the pictures to avoid her gaze. "Deserve what?"

"Your disregard. I'm trying to be your friend but you're making it pretty darned difficult."

"Don't need a friend," he said. "I need to be left alone."

She shoved back from the table and stood. "Sure you do. That's the way you operate, isn't it? Always the tough guy. But let me tell you something, Dallas Calloway. A future with the prospect of happiness is a terrible thing to squander, and you're the one who's afraid of getting hurt, not me."

Without awaiting his response, she rushed out the door and slammed it behind her. She despised the overwhelming disappointment. Hated that she couldn't reach him and probably never would. Most important, she detested the emotions welling inside her. She couldn't save him from himself and for some reason that made her so sad.

Somehow, someway, she had come perilously close to falling in love with the wounded cowboy, or at least the one she'd known while they were away. If she let the cycle complete, she would most surely collide head-on with devastation.

To prevent that from happening, and for self-protection, she would let Dallas continue to brood, and in the meantime, she would get out of his bed. But as far as their arrangement went, she vowed to see it through. No matter how hard he might try to drive her away, she wasn't going to budge until she saw the arrangement through.

When he retired at midnight, Dallas found nothing but a deserted room and an empty bed. He also discovered all her clothes were gone, and the toiletries, too. Not one sign that Paris had ever been in his life.

Unexpected panic set in and sent him to the garage first, where he found the Mercedes parked next to the truck. That didn't mean she hadn't abandoned the car and found another way to leave him.

He wouldn't blame her if she'd left. He'd been a moody bastard and he'd pushed her away. He couldn't stand the thought of her taking off without telling him goodbye. Taking off at all.

He took the stairs two at a time, flipped on the hallway lights and started opening doors to the additional rooms. By the time he reached the final one at the end of the corridor, he'd all but given up…until he found her in the black sleigh bed wearing a pink nightshirt, a pillow propped behind her back, her legs crossed before her and a computer in her lap.

"Mind if I come in?"

"Depends on why you're here," she said without taking her attention from the laptop.

"I'm here to talk."

Finally she looked up. "Wow. That's new and different. Are you ill?"

Sick over hurting her feelings. He perched on the edge of the mattress near the footboard and sighed.

"First, I want to say I'm sorry. You're right, I haven't been treating you well and it's not fair. My problems aren't your fault."

"Apology accepted. Go on."

"Secondly, I suck at being a boyfriend."

That made her laugh. "In case you've forgotten, we kind of skipped the boyfriend-girlfriend stage and went right to the marriage. Besides, I wasn't looking for a boyfriend when I entered into this mess."

The "mess" thing didn't bode well for him. "Okay, I suck at relationships. And I didn't come looking for you, either. But here you are, and honestly, it does scare me."

She closed the computer and set it aside. "Why?"

Now for the admission he didn't count on making. "Because I do care about you, Paris. I don't think I realized how much until I thought you'd left."

"I promised you I'd stay until the bitter end."

"And I promised you an annulment."

"As I've previously stated, that was due to faulty research and an unreasonable timeline."

"Do you regret marrying me?"

She paused for a few seconds. "I regret that more couldn't exist between us aside from you keeping the ranch and me alleviating my debt. But hey, I'm a realist. This is a unique situation. I don't regret our time at the cabin, even if it was only temporary and apparently over."

"It doesn't have to be."

She frowned. "All signs point to the contrary, Dallas. I refuse to make love to a man who won't give me the time of day."

"What if I try to do better?" He drew in a breath and released it slowly. "What if I told you I want to see where this thing goes between us in the next year?"

He green eyes widened. "Do you mean exploring the possibility of making it permanent?"

"Yeah. There's no guarantee it will work, but I'd like to try. It would require starting over, since we put the cart before the horse."

"You mean like dating?"

"I guess you could call it that. I want to take you out to dinner and maybe go see a movie or two. I definitely want to teach you how to ride if you're going to be a rancher's wife."

She held up her hands, palms forward. "Wait a minute. I'm still trying to digest the whole dating thing."

So was he. "Okay. I'll slow down. But just so you know, I've never had a relationship that lasted longer than six months. Maybe that's because I don't know what it takes."

Paris unfolded her legs, draped them over the bed and scooted next to him. "My mother always said that when you evaluate who you're going to have as a life partner, you have to ask yourself, *Will they make me a better person?*"

Solid advice. "I believe that could be true when it comes to you making me a better man. You'd probably be getting the short end of the stick with me."

She hooked her arm through his and kissed his cheek. "I think we could make each other better."

For the first time in two weeks, he felt optimistic

and not quite as afraid of making her life miserable. "As long as we both can trust each other."

"We can do that."

"Can we still have sex while we're dating?"

That earned him a mild punch in the biceps and her smile. "Is that all you men think about?"

"Pretty much."

She released an exaggerated sigh. "Oh, all right. I suppose we can tango between the sheets now and then."

He came to his feet, ready for the dance to begin. "Let's get back to our bedroom, wife."

She stood, grabbed the nightshirt's hem and pulled it over her head. "We have a perfectly good bed here, husband, so let's mix it up."

Up would be the operative word when she slid her panties down and tossed them onto the nearby chair. "You won't catch me arguing with a naked woman."

Dallas undressed in a rush, took her down on the bed, kissed her thoroughly and then sent his lips and hands on a mission over her body. She responded strongly to his touch and climaxed quickly beneath his mouth. He realized he didn't have a condom, but this time he didn't care. He trusted Paris completely, not to mention he'd seen her birth control pills.

When he started to move over her, Paris said, "Not this time," before nudging him onto his back. "I want to play cowgirl."

Damned if she wasn't full of surprises. "Lady, ride away. I just hope this lasts longer than eight seconds."

It took all his strength to hold back the orgasm when

she climbed on top and guided him inside her. Having no barriers between them only increased the sensations, and he realized he'd never had sex without protection, a lesson that had been drilled into his brain by his dad. The wait had been worth it. But it also happened to be playing hell with his control, and no matter how hard he tried to hold back the tide, the dam broke all too soon.

After Paris collapsed against him, Dallas rubbed her back and felt a strong sense of peace, like this is where they belonged. Like the way love might feel.

Whoa. He sure as hell wasn't going to go there yet.

"Did you enjoy that?" Paris whispered in his ear.

"Hell yeah. I always like new adventures."

She lifted her head and smiled. "So do I."

He brushed her hair away from her cheek. "Darlin', get ready for all the adventure you can handle."

For the past three weeks, the adventures had kept coming like hits on a radio. She'd learned to ride a horse—kind of—spent three days holed up in a cabin in Wyoming with Dallas and attended a country music award ceremony on his arm in Nashville.

Paris couldn't remember when she'd had so much fun, or so much fantastic sex. No place had been off-limits, from hot tubs to home-theater chairs to pickup trucks. And yesterday, when she'd walked in the office to show Dallas the latest plans for the lodge, she ended up with her dress hiked up to her waist and her panties down at her ankles while her husband ravished her on his desk without taking off his boots.

Memories of those moments brought about a blush

when she returned to the office today and came face-to-face with both the mothers. "It sure is getting hotter outside," she said as she entered the opening at the counter.

"Hotter inside, too," Maria muttered while Jenny giggled. "Real hot yesterday."

Mortified, Paris rushed toward Dallas's study, hurried inside, closed the door behind her and leaned back against it. "They know."

Dallas glanced up from a document and frowned. "Know what?"

She walked to his desk and collapsed into the chair. "They know what we did in here yesterday."

"Why do you say that?"

"Because Maria just made a comment about it being hot inside when I said it was hot outside." She snapped a finger and pointed. "You pressed the intercom and told Jenny to hold all your calls and I bet the button got stuck. You need to get that fixed before we do it in here again."

He grinned. "Darlin', are you ready for another round?"

Yes. "No. I came here to tell you to schedule the groundbreaking for the lodge next week. I've been working with the architect and we've almost finalized the design. If you have a few minutes, I want to fill you in on the details."

He stood and rounded the desk. "We might not be ready to build yet, but that's still cause for celebration."

When he bent down and nibbled her ear, Paris shivered. "Stop it, you bad, bad cowboy, and let your fake wife tell you about the lodge."

He pulled her out of her chair and brought her into his arms. "You like me when I'm bad, Mrs. Calloway."

"And you like me bad, too, Mr. Calloway."

"That I do."

Just as Dallas planted his mouth on hers for a hair-curling kiss, the pesky intercom sounded. When the buzz repeated twice, Paris pulled back. "Aren't you going to answer that?"

"Do I have to?"

"It could be important."

He looked thoroughly put out. "You're right. I have an appointment in about fifteen minutes with a supplier. He's probably early, dammit."

She stood on tiptoe and kissed his chin. "I suppose I'll see you at the house for dinner."

"Yep, and when I get there, be naked."

"I can do that."

He let her go to depress the pesky button. "Yeah, Jen."

"There's someone here to see your wife."

Dallas sent her a confused look, prompting Paris to say, "I'm not expecting anyone."

"Who is it, Jen?" he asked.

"Maybe she should just come out here, sugar."

"A name, Jen," Dallas said. "Stop beatin' around the bush."

"He says he's her husband."

Nine

From the panic on Paris's face, Dallas figured she hadn't expected this blast from her past. "What the hell does he want?"

"I have no idea," she said as she started toward the door. "But I'm going to find out."

"Don't go out there," he said as he pushed the button. "Send him in, Jen."

When she spun, fear flashed in her eyes. "I need to handle this myself."

"Fine, but I want to be there when you do." In case he needed to take matters into his own hands with the bastard.

The loud rap obviously startled Paris, sending her around to open the door to a lanky, blond-haired guy wearing a prissy pink polo shirt, chinos and a smirk. "Hello, Paris."

"Hello, jerk."

Dallas wanted to applaud when the idiot reached for her and she sidestepped him. He also wanted to punch the guy and wasn't ruling that out.

Paris held on to the doorframe but didn't invite him into the room. "Why are you here?"

He leaned over and eyed Dallas. "I have information that would interest you and your new *husband*." He had the nerve to push past Paris, stride to the desk and stick out a bony hand. "It's a pleasure to meet the other husband."

Dallas ignored the gesture. "Pleasure's all mine, Dick."

"It's Peter."

"Whatever. Now state your business and get the hell out of here."

The bastard dropped his arm and sneered. "You might not be so quick to dismiss me once I say what I have to say."

He fought the urge to wrap a hand around that skinny neck and toss him out. "Hurry up."

"Dallas, could I have a few moments alone with him?" Paris asked.

No way. No how. "Not on your life, sweetheart. But I am going to step out and tell Jen to reschedule my appointment." He intended to tell her more than that. "In the meantime, don't say anything to him until I get back."

He hated to leave Paris alone, but he didn't trust the

son of a bitch or his motives. For that reason, he strode to the reception area and gestured Jen aside. "Do you still have that digital recorder?"

She looked a little clueless. "Yes. Why?"

"Because as soon as I get back in there, I want you to turn it on and press the intercom. Can you handle that?"

"Of course."

"Good. I also want you to go outside, call the sheriff on your cell phone and have him send a deputy over to be on standby."

Now she looked alarmed. "Are you afraid he's going to harm you, sugar?"

"No. I'm afraid I might hurt him. And I'm also thinking he might be up to no good."

He turned around to head back to the office and hoped like hell Jen followed his instructions to a tee. If the bastard tried to pull anything at all, at least they'd have proof and the law on their side.

When he entered the room, he found Paris seated in the chair under the window while the ex roosted in the one across from the desk. They both sat silent like they'd been engaged in a standoff.

Dallas decided to stand next to his wife. "Okay, the floor's yours, Pete," he said. "Have at it."

The guy crossed one leg over the other, looking every bit the wimp he was. "How much do you know about Paris, Mr. Calloway?"

"All that I need to know," he answered before Paris could open her mouth.

"Then she told you about her criminal history."

"I don't have a criminal history," Paris shot back. "I covered for yours."

Dallas didn't care for where this was heading. "What is he talking about, Paris?"

"He embezzled funds from our former employer," she said. "He led them to believe it was all my idea, which it was not. I'm only guilty of being gullible and stupid."

The SOB let go a grating laugh. "Don't play innocent, Paris. You had no problem spending the funds that I borrowed from the company."

"You mean stole, don't you?" Paris scooted up to the edge of the chair. "I didn't have time to spend a dime other than what we needed for bills. I was too busy working. You, on the other hand, were hitting on every woman in Vegas. They reaped the benefits of your ill-begotten gains and now I'm charged with paying off your debt or risk going to jail."

Dallas wasn't at all pleased that Paris had withheld this level of information. "Looks like I'm a walking example of 'the husband is the last to know.'"

"About that husband thing," Peter chimed in. "There's a bit of a problem with that."

Dallas leveled his gaze on the bastard. "What kind of problem?"

"Paris and I are still married."

A strong wave of nausea hit Paris, driving her to take a few calming breaths before she could respond. "I don't understand."

"It's simple," Peter said. "I didn't complete the divorce process in the Dominican Republic for leverage."

Dallas released a few unflattering oaths aimed at the once-believed-to-be-ex-husband. He then turned his obvious anger on her. "You told me you had the documents, Paris."

She'd never felt so hopeless, or foolish, in her life. "I did. I do."

Peter's laugh sounded maniacal. "Since I knew you know very little Spanish, I sent you a record of a civil lawsuit that I obtained from the internet and I altered a photo of the official record from the Dominican Republic to include our names. You should have hired an attorney to protect your interests, dear. You did have that option."

She had the strongest urge to dump him out of the chair. How could she have been so blind to believe he was a decent guy when she'd married him? Easy. He'd been a chameleon and a con, and she'd been a naive girl. "I spent all the money I had left on attorney fees to stay out of jail, all because of you."

"Someday perhaps you will learn not to be so trusting, Paris."

She had another urge to slap that condescending grin off his face but settled for a verbal slug. "You should get help for your short man's syndrome, although it does apply in every sense of the word, you miscreant con artist."

Dallas took a step toward Peter. "You could've told her this in a phone call, which leads me to believe you're up to something."

"I considered calling," he replied. "But I couldn't be certain she would tell you everything."

Paris shot out of the chair. "You're the liar, not me."

"What do you want?" Dallas asked, his fists balled at his sides.

"Well, for starters," Peter began, "I'm sure you wouldn't want this scandalous secret to taint your good name. If you give me fifty thousand dollars, I won't go to the media and tell them you married another man's wife. A hundred thousand buys Paris a proper and legal divorce so you two can resume your life together."

Before Paris could react, Dallas had Peter by the collar and backed up to the wall. "Listen, you son of a bitch, I strongly suggest you take your blackmail attempts and get the hell out of here before I forget there's a lady present and I throw you out the window."

For the first time she saw fear in Peter's eyes. "It's your choice. If I don't have the money by tomorrow, in cash, I will notify the press. As far as the divorce is concerned, it's immaterial to me what you do. It's no skin off my nose to stay married to the most gullible woman I've ever known."

Dallas balled his fist but before he could throw a punch, someone said, "Don't do it, Calloway, or I'll have to arrest you, too."

Paris looked straight ahead to see a deputy filling the doorframe, Jenny cowering behind him.

Dallas shoved Peter toward the officer. "Did you get it all recorded?" he asked Jenny.

"Every bit, sugar."

He addressed the deputy then. "Did you hear it, Rowdy?"

The man patted his rounded belly. "Every word, Dallas."

The deputy stepped toward Peter and withdrew a pair of handcuffs. "Turn around and put your hands behind your back."

Peter stood in stunned silence for a few seconds. "Why are you arresting me? He should be cuffed for assault."

"I don't see any signs of assault," Rowdy said as he turned him around and snapped the cuffs into place. "You, my man, are in a heap of hot water."

Peter shot a menacing look in Paris's direction. "What are the charges?"

"Extortion. Embezzlement," Rowdy answered. "Take your pick. You want me to lock him up, Dallas?"

"Not yet." He stared at Peter for a long moment. "I'll make you a deal, Pete. If you never show your face here again, I'll let you slide for now. But if I ever lay eyes on your sorry self, and if I learn you uttered one word about this to even the clerk at the convenience store, I'll have you thrown in jail so fast your head will spin. I'll also play your confession to your former boss."

Peter practically cowered. "All right."

"And as far as that divorce goes," Dallas continued, "I want you back on a plane to finish the procedure and I plan to hire that lawyer to make sure you follow through this time. Understand?"

"Yes, I understand."

"Good. Rowdy, get him out of my sight before I forget why I didn't coldcock him the minute he opened his mouth."

As the deputy led Peter away, Paris waited for the shock to subside before facing Dallas again. "I am so, so sorry."

His somber expression spoke volumes. "Sorry about which part? That we're not legally married or that you lied to me about your past?"

She should have seen this coming. "I didn't exactly lie about the theft at the firm since I legally couldn't tell you. When Peter left the country before he could answer to the allegations, both parties signed a nondisclosure in exchange for my agreement to pay off the debt. My former employer was convinced I played some role, but I swear I didn't."

"You mean to tell me that you lived and worked with the man and you didn't know a damn thing about it?"

His distrust burned like a hot poker to the heart, though she couldn't exactly blame him under the circumstances. "I didn't have a clue because we had separate checking accounts. He was double billing vendors and depositing the excess in various places. Of course, he did give me funds to pay his half of the bills, so in essence I did benefit from his illegal activities, but I didn't know that's what I was doing."

Skeptical would be the best way to describe the look Dallas gave her. "Well, darlin', at least you won't have to worry about getting our divorce now. You're free to go do what you please."

She expected him to be angry. Livid even. But not to be totally written off. "You're being unreasonable."

"I'm being practical."

His attitude absolutely floored her. "Look, I understand why you're upset. I even understand why you might question my role in the embezzlement. But I can't quite comprehend after all we've been through why you can't give me the benefit of the doubt when I afforded you that courtesy over the annulment issue. I've never given you any reason not to trust me."

"You just did, by deceiving me. Lying by omission is as bad as a bald-face lie."

She truly wanted to scream. "So that's it? All the time we've spent together means nothing?"

"If you're worried about losing the money I fronted you, keep it. Keep the car, too, since I sold the old one for scrap. I'll even give you a good reference for what you've already accomplished on the lodge design."

"I don't want your money or the car or the job. I also don't want any more of your excuses."

"Excuses?"

"You've been looking for an out and I handed it to you on a silver platter. In fact, you lied to me when you said you wanted to see where our relationship might go. You never had any intention of making this marriage work. You only told me that to keep me in your bed."

"That's not true, Paris."

"Oh, really? Well, listen up, cowboy. You were right when you said you don't know how to commit because committed couples weather the storms and forgive all the flaws. But then you don't know the first thing about forgiveness because you certainly haven't forgiven your father. Since he's a blood relative, and I'm little more than your playmate, I don't stand a chance."

Before she started to cry, she had to leave. But she still had one more thing to tell him. "Even after knowing what I know about you now, I still believe in you, because Dallas, I've fallen in love with you although that's the last thing I wanted to do. I only wish you believed in me, too. I'll be out of here tonight." She removed the wedding band from her finger and laid it on the desk. "Have a nice life."

As she walked away, tears began to flow, yet she managed to get outside before the dam completely burst. She left the Mercedes parked in front of the office and started to the house on foot, hoping that maybe Dallas would come to his senses and come after her. But by the time she reached the front door, she realized that wasn't going to happen.

Now all she had left were the memories, a few mementos, some money and a severely shattered heart.

"What in the hell are you doing, *mijo*?"

An hour after the sorry scene, Dallas turned from the office window to see the mothers filing into the room, led by Maria, along with a band of merry brothers. All his brothers—Austin, Tyler, Houston, Worth—except one. Judges and jury members all wrapped into one family unit, thanks to his matriarchs' role as family criers.

"Why are you all here?"

"We're here to talk to you about Paris," Maria answered.

Figured. "Nothing to talk about, so you can leave and take the boys with you."

"We've filled them all in on the details, sugar," Jen said. "We're worried about you."

He had a good mind to walk out before the show started, but they'd probably follow him. "If you're going to take turns taking potshots and me, that's the last thing I need at the moment."

Austin stepped forward first. "I'd personally like to knock some sense into you. Do you have any idea what you've done to that little gal?"

"He's stomped on her heart," Tyler replied for Dallas. "I saw her walking up the road, crying like a baby."

"And now he's lost the ranch in the process," Worth added.

Houston took a step forward. "Hell, Dallas, Fort is going to have a field day with this once he knows you're no longer married."

Dallas had about had enough. "We weren't married in the first place, dammit, and that's not my fault."

"It's not Paris's fault either, sugar," Jenny chimed in. "She was victimized by a man and the fact that you dismissed her so easily means you've done the same thing to her."

He hadn't done that. Or had he? "You all know how much I hate deception. She could've told me what happened with her former employer because I wouldn't have told a soul. I didn't have to hear it from that SOB ex-husband. Oh, yeah. Her current husband."

"And you're so damned perfect, Dallas," Austin added. "You tossed her out before you gave her a chance."

His temper was close to reaching the boiling point. "And you're a damned hypocrite, Austin. You were married to Lilly, what, less than a year?"

Austin looked like he wanted to throw a left hook. "At least I made it to a year. Plus we both decided the marriage wasn't working."

"That's what happens when you get drunk and get hitched."

"Kiss my—"

Maria clapped her hands and pointed toward the door. "Everyone out. This kangaroo court is dismissed."

"Yes, boys, you should all go because we need to talk to Dallas alone," Jenny said.

Maria scowled. "When I said everyone, that means you, too, Jenny. I'm going to handle this."

Jenny looked dejected. "But—"

"No buts. Go."

After the crowd disappeared, Maria gestured toward the desk chair. "Sit down, *mijo*, and I'm going to tell you how the cow ate the cabbage."

Great. Just great. "I'd rather go work off some steam in the barn."

"I don't care what you want, Dallas Calloway. You're going to hear me out. *Comprendes?*"

He understood all too well. He was about to get a butt chewing. "Fine. But make it fast."

Maria took a seat in front of the desk. "I will make it very fast because you're running out of time. If you don't get your head on straight, Paris is going to leave and she won't be coming back."

The thought left a bitter taste in his mouth even though it's what he wanted. Or what he thought he wanted. "The damage is done and it can't be repaired, Mom."

"Love fixes anything."

That nearly shocked him out of his boots. "I've never said I love her."

"I'm sure you haven't, but that doesn't mean you don't. I've seen the way you look at her, *mijo*."

"You're seeing lust."

"Like hell I am. I've lived long enough to know the difference. She walks in the room and you hang on her every word. You open doors for her and you put your hand on her back when you're walking out together. You always let her speak without interrupting and you're always asking if she needs anything, and I don't mean sex. I've even heard you say hurry back if you're watching TV and she goes into the kitchen."

"And your point?"

Maria muttered a few choice words in her native tongue. Words he'd learned from some of the hands. "Let me ask you something. Do you wake up every morning thinking about her and go to bed every night glad she's going to be by your side?"

As bad as he hated to admit it, all that was true. "Yeah."

"Do you imagine growing old with her?"

Damn. "Maybe."

"Do you wonder what it would be like if she had your babies?"

"I've always made it clear I don't want kids."

"Answer me."

He released a rough sigh. "Not at first, but lately, yeah."

"Have you ever felt this way about any other woman?"

The answer was easy, and pretty damn telling. "Nope."

Maria slapped her palms on the desk and stood. "You're in love, although you're too damn hardheaded to admit it to yourself. If you don't get to the house, get on your knees and beg Paris for forgiveness for being a *cobarde*, you're going to live the rest of your life with a belly full of regrets. She'll forever be known to you as the one who got away when she should be the one who saved you from one helluva lonely life."

Deep down he recognized everything Maria had said made sense. He also realized he had one major problem. "What if she doesn't accept my apology?"

"She will if you offer her the ring."

He didn't have to ask which ring. The one meant for his true love. And damned if he hadn't found her. But... "You think it's a good idea I propose?"

"Do you still want to marry her?"

Did horses like hay? "Yeah."

"Then I'll go get the ring, and you go get the girl."

Ten

"Sugar, are you sure you can't wait until the morning before you go?"

Paris kept right on packing. And sniffling. And occasionally sobbing. "He doesn't want me here, Jenny, so the faster I leave, the better it will be for all concerned, myself included."

"Not as far as we're all concerned," Jenny said. "You should have seen the boys take him on for his cruelty. I thought Austin and Dallas were going to actually fight."

Wherever she went, clearly trouble followed. "I'm sorry this has caused a divide in the family. I never meant for that to happen."

Jenny handed her a tissue. "Honey, none of this is your fault. If Dallas wasn't so darned pigheaded, he'd realize you had no choice but to lie. He would also realize what the two of you have together is worth fighting for."

"You can't fight for something you don't care to win. Dallas has already decided what he wants, and it's not me. I need to be with someone who's willing to accept me for who I am, an imperfect woman."

"Sugar, he believes in you. He just doesn't believe in himself."

After dabbing at her eyes, Paris zipped the last suitcase and set it next to the other two at the foot of the bed. "Dallas hates deception, justified or not. And he doesn't feel he's capable of a long-term commitment. He has his father to thank for that. No offense."

"Oh, sugar, we all know J.D. was a lying philanderer, but we loved him all the same."

"That's because you know how to forgive. Dallas hasn't learned that lesson yet."

"Dallas hasn't figured out everyone lies now and then. Why, my mother passed herself off for years as the consummate Southern lady when in fact she grew up in the Bronx. She got away with it because she mastered the accent perfectly. And she learned how to make those luscious mint juleps. Would you like me to make you one before you go?"

It would only delay her departure if she passed out. "No, thank you, but if you could call a cab I would definitely appreciate it."

"Dallas bought you a perfectly good car."

"I don't want it." She didn't want anything more from him aside from some good memories to override the bad.

"Honey, there aren't any cabs that come out here. But

I would be glad to drive you anywhere you want to go, although I don't see why you won't take the Mercedes since it was a gift from Dallas."

A gift that came with conditions—marry me, make love with me but don't get too close. "He can give it to the next faux bride. I'm sure he'll get to work on that first thing in the morning, before Fort finds out we aren't married."

Jenny drew her into a hug. "I promise you, he won't go looking for someone else. Besides, the birthday deadline has passed, not to mention he doesn't want anyone but you."

If only that were true. "He doesn't want me, Jenny. I'm no longer of any use to him."

"I guess we'll see, won't we?" She sounded as if she knew a secret.

Paris pulled the handles from the rolling bags and slid the duffel's strap over her shoulder. "I won't see anything since I'm ready to go. If you could just drop me off in the nearest town, I'll find a room and rent a car tomorrow." At least she had enough money to get her to Idaho to stay with her parents and explain once again how she'd been duped by another man. Oh, joy.

Jenny gave her a pretend pout. "Are you sure you won't change your mind about that drink? Or how about some dinner? I could make you a nice vegetable frittata."

Her stomach roiled over the thought of choking down any food. "You've done enough already. And by the way, Dallas has enough money to hire a private chef, so why doesn't he?"

"Because he knows I like to make sure all the boys are fed. It makes me feel useful."

Unbelievable. "You make dinner for the other four?"

"Almost every night unless they're out of town or engaged in activities with women that no mother should be exposed to. Which is sometimes quite often with Worth. That little apple didn't fall far from the family tree."

They shared a laugh and another hug before heading out of the bedroom…and running right into none other than her erstwhile pretend husband. Her heart sank a little over the sight of him, and the regrets tugged at her soul.

When Paris muttered an apology and tried to push past him, he clasped her arm, halting her progress. "We need to talk."

"I think we've said all we have to say. No need to belabor the point and my shortcomings."

Jenny took the duffel from Paris. "Hear him out, sugar."

Maria appeared in the hall to give her two cents worth. "It's important, *mija*. Let's go to the kitchen, Jenny."

"No, stay," Dallas said. "I don't care if the whole damn county hears this, as long as the two of you don't interrupt. Besides, you're going to eavesdrop anyway."

Paris wasn't at all certain how to take any of this. "Then make it quick so I can get out of here."

"I don't want you to go. It's going to kill me if you go."

A stunning development. "I can't stay with a man who can't trust me, Dallas."

"I trust you, darlin'. I don't always trust me. But I'm going to learn if it's the last thing I do. And you were right, I got cold feet and blamed you for it."

Oh, how she wanted to believe him. "If that's the case, why the sudden change of heart?"

He looked somewhat sheepish. "I had a little help with that."

"From me," Maria stated without regard for the non-interruption directive. "I verbally beat him over the head."

"She just said things that made sense," he countered. "She made me take inventory of my feelings for you, and it led to a fairly obvious conclusion."

"Which is?"

"I love you, sweetheart."

She lost her grip on the bags' handles, sending the upright suitcases onto the floor. "Could you repeat that, please?"

He circled his arms around her. "I love you more than this ranch. More than I ever thought I could love anyone. We'll find our own place and build a house, along with a future together."

"And we'll all go with you if we have to," Jenny said.

"Don't give her any reason not to stay with him," Maria scolded.

She let that proposition soak in for a moment. "I love you, too, but is that enough?"

"It's a start. And we won't know unless you stay."

"You do realize we're not married anymore and it's bound to get out."

"We can fix that real quick." He pulled a blue velvet

box from his shirt pocket, opened it to reveal a gorgeous marquise diamond that had to be at least two carats and lowered to one knee. "Paris, this belonged to my mom and it was given to me to give to the woman I want to spend my life with. That woman is you. So will you marry me again and have our babies and make this miserable cowboy a better man?"

Paris stood there, mouth agape, basking in the emotion in his eyes, the sincerity in his words, until reality jumped into the euphoria. "I'm not divorced yet."

"We don't have to be in a hurry. We're going to need time to plan a proper wedding anyway."

"I can't wait," Jenny practically shouted.

A proper wedding would be wonderful. However, another issue still remained. "But you'll lose the D Bar C if Fort finds out we're not married anymore. Maybe we should hurry up and do it."

"I don't care about Fort or the will. I only want to be with you. This isn't about keeping the ranch—it's about keeping you close, always."

As much as she wanted to accept his heartfelt proposal, she still had one more question. "You're serious about wanting babies?"

"Yep. I actually like them. I help with the rodeo club at the local high school and I plan to have a summer riding camp for the younger ones. If I can ride a bull, I can take on a baby. Or babies."

Paris managed a smile around the mist forming in her eyes. "As long as you don't expect us to keep them in the barn."

"I promise. And by the way, I have a bum knee,

thanks to a rank horse that bucked me off two years ago, so if you could give me an answer, my joints would appreciate it."

She laughed through the tears. "Yes, I will marry you, bad knees and all, so you can get up now."

After sliding the ring on her finger, Dallas rose and drew her into a soft kiss. "We're going to have a lot of adventures. And when we find our own place, you can design the house to your liking."

"Actually, you probably won't have to move after all, sugar."

Dallas let her go long enough to stare at Jenny. "Fort will probably say otherwise."

She shook her head. "No, he won't. I told him if he wouldn't pursue the terms of the will, I'd give him my half of the horse farm in Louisiana."

"I thought you'd already done that," Dallas said.

Jenny grinned. "I conveniently forgot to do it, just in case I need some leverage, even though he didn't know that. Sometimes you just have to tell a little white lie."

"When did this happen?" Paris asked.

Jenny stared at her pink peep-toe pumps. "The day you arrived here after the wedding. I had a feeling you two would be a good fit if given the chance. Also, around these parts, available women are few and far between."

"And you just let the marriage plans go on without telling me?" Both his tone and expression revealed Dallas's displeasure.

Jenny propped her hands on her hips. "Yes, sugar, and you should thank your lucky stars I didn't tell you.

Otherwise, you wouldn't be engaged to the woman of your dreams."

Dallas turned his attention to Maria. "Did you know, too?"

"Yep. I figured it was the only way to get you hitched so you can have me some grandbabies."

He pointed to the hall behind him. "Both of you can leave now."

Ignoring the order, Maria gave Paris a hug. "Welcome to the family, *mija*. Get ready for one wild ride."

After Jenny and Maria departed, Dallas pulled Paris back into his arms. "Looks like everything is going to work out after all. I keep the ranch and the girl. Who would've guessed that would happen?"

Not Paris. Not in a million years. "Did you know I almost decided to settle in New York? If I had, we would never have met."

"What changed your mind?"

"Actually, I'd picked out an apartment to rent and the landlord decided to sell it right before I left Vegas. Then I turned on my computer to search for another one, and I saw an ad for San Antonio. Something told me I needed to be in Texas, and here I am with my very own cowboy whom I love with all my heart."

He kissed her again, a little longer and deeper this time. "Care to take that cowboy and show him how much you love him?"

"I'll race you to the bedroom."

"Who said anything about the bedroom?"

"We're not going to do it here in the hall, Dallas. Not

with the probability that Jenny and Maria are somewhere nearby."

"True, and we're going to set some ground rules
about that. But I'm actually thinking I want to make
love to you in a place we haven't tried yet."

Paris tapped her chin with a fingertip and pretended
to think. "I can't recall a place where we haven't done
it."

"It's the place where we won't be keeping the kids."

They exchanged a smile and simultaneously said,
"The barn."

Most women wouldn't agree to get hitched in front
of a barn. But Paris Reynolds Calloway wasn't most
women, Dallas decided. She'd turned out to be one in
a million, and now she belonged to him. And he definitely belonged to her.

He stood next to Maria, choking down one of Jenny's
gut-burning brews so he wouldn't hurt her feelings, even
if he preferred beer. As he watched Paris visiting with
her parents beneath the tent's canopy, he noticed she'd
only been drinking punch.

"She looks beautiful, *mijo*. And very happy."

"Yeah, she does." When he'd seen Paris coming
down the makeshift aisle an hour ago, wearing that
form-fitting, long, sleeveless silk gown, sparkling tiny
flowers sprinkled through her hair, he couldn't believe
he'd gotten so lucky. "Her folks seem fairly nice, too."

"Her dad's a piece of work," she said. "He told me
he brought a shotgun in case you bowed out. I told him
I had one handy, too."

Dallas couldn't help but laugh over the image of his stepmom wielding a weapon while wearing a dress. "In-laws and outlaws. Works for me."

At that moment, Paris caught his eye, smiled and started toward him. Once she arrived, he leaned over and kissed her. "Do you think we can have a few minutes alone before dinner is served?"

"I'm going now," Maria said. "I've got to make sure Jen isn't putting too much tequila in those drinks."

After his mom disappeared into the tent, Dallas wrapped his arms around his wife. "How are you holding up?"

"Pretty well for a woman who planned a wedding in less than two months."

"Any regrets so far?"

"No, other than we have to wait another four hours or so before we can start the honeymoon. Actually, second honeymoon. And speaking of that, are you going to tell me where you're taking me?"

"I'll give you a hint. It involves a boat."

"The cabin?"

"No. It involves a big boat. Worth offered his yacht with a full crew and captain. I figure we can mosey on down to the Mexican Caribbean for two weeks where I've rented a private villa."

She hugged him hard and kissed him soundly. "That sounds wonderful, honey."

"And since I'm not getting any younger, I also figure we can get on with the baby-making."

She glanced at the ground before raising her gaze

to his. "Now that you mention it, I probably should tell you it's too late for that."

For a second he couldn't speak. "How? When?"

"Well, *how* is pretty obvious, although exactly where is up for grabs. I estimate it happened around six weeks ago. And in case you're wondering why, it's been crazy with the wedding plans and I might have missed a pill or two. But I swear on my mother's favorite blue flats, which she's wearing now, I did not plan this."

He waited for the urge to head for the hills, but it didn't come. He might be a bit nervous, but he wasn't spooked. "I believe you, darlin'. And I'm looking forward to being a dad."

She immediately relaxed. "I am so glad. I wasn't sure how I was going to tell you after I confirmed it this morning."

"This morning?"

"Yes. I looked at the calendar on my phone and thought something's missing, and it ain't only my mind."

"Ain't? Looks like you're picking up the cowboy vernacular. I'm impressed."

"Vernacular? Now I'm impressed."

"Hey, I might be a hayseed, but I have a little class in me, too. I also have a hankering to kiss my bride and the mother of my baby."

She draped her arms around his neck. "Kiss away, cowboy."

Before he could, he felt a tap on his shoulder and turned to find his brother standing there. "What do you want, Austin?"

"We want you both in the tent for a toast."

"Are you going to make it?"

"Nope. Worth drew the shortest straw."

Paris laughed. "This should be interesting."

"Or a train wreck," Dallas said.

When they walked beneath the canopy, Dallas spotted his youngest brother standing on the stage reserved for the band, Jenny standing at his side. A roving waiter offered them champagne, which Paris nixed for a glass of water, while Dallas picked up a flute.

Worth held his glass up and cleared his throat. "To my brother Dallas, who had the good sense to wed a woman like Paris. And to my new sister-in-law, I hope you own a pair of boots because he'll probably have you muck the stalls before you know it. Best of luck to you both and may your trail ride together be a long one."

After the applause died down, Dallas put down the wine and grabbed his wife's hand to lead her to the stage.

"Dallas, what are we doing?" she asked once they reached their destination.

"You'll see." He circled his arm around her waist and prepared to say a few words. "We'd like to thank all you folks for sharing in this day with us. I'd also like to thank Jen for pulling together one heck of a party in a short amount of time, and my mom, Maria, for being there for me through thick or thin after I lost my own mother. If my dad were here, he'd pat me on the back and tell me *You did good, son*, and I did." He looked into Paris's eyes and saw honest-to-goodness love there. "And Paris, I never expected to find someone as special as you, and I sure as hell never really thought I'd settle down, but I'm damn glad I did. Thank you for honoring me with your vows, and for carrying our baby."

That caused a spattering of gasps among the onlookers and another toast from Houston. "To the Calloway sperm, known for being good swimmers."

"And I hope it's not catching," Tyler said, spurring a lot of laughter in the crowd.

Dallas guided Paris through the maze of guests offering their congratulations and managed to get her alone again, this time in the barn. "I hope you don't mind me telling everyone," he told her after they arrived. "I just couldn't wait to let everyone know."

"It's okay," she said. "I would have liked to have waited a little while since it's so early."

He held her again. "Darlin', I will do everything in my power to protect you. I promise you won't have to muck any stalls and I'll make sure you stay off your feet and get plenty of rest—"

She pressed a fingertip to his lips. "I'm having a baby, honey, not suffering from an incurable illness. Women do it every day. And I just know everything will turn out well with our little girl."

"Or boy."

She sighed. "You're probably right if you inherited the Calloway sperm that not only swims fast, it produces male children."

"Stranger things have happened. After all, the woman of my dreams said yes."

"Twice," she said. "And I am so glad I did. I love you, Mr. Calloway."

"I love you, too, Mrs. Calloway."

Maybe he had too much pride and too many trust issues. Maybe he still had a lot of learning to do about love, women, and most of all, himself. But with Paris by his side, Dallas felt confident he would master those lessons in time. One thing he did know for sure, when this beautiful blonde breezed through his door three months ago, that turned out to be the best day of his life. He expected to have many, many more.

* * * * *

*If you loved this novel,
check out these other sexy reads from
Kristi Gold*

*THE RETURN OF THE SHEIKH
ONE NIGHT WITH THE SHEIKH
THE SHEIKH'S SON
ONE HOT DESERT NIGHT
THE SHEIKH'S SECRET HEIR*

All available now, only from Harlequin Desire!

***

*If you're on Twitter, tell us what you think of
Harlequin Desire! #harlequindesire*

COMING NEXT MONTH FROM

HARLEQUIN

Desire

Available April 5, 2016

#2437 TAKE ME, COWBOY
Copper Ridge • by Maisey Yates
Tomboy Anna Brown *wants* to tap into her femininity, but is clueless on *how* to do so. When her brothers bet she'll be dateless at a charity auction, she turns to a makeover—and her way-too-sexy best friend— to prove them wrong.

#2438 HIS BABY AGENDA
Billionaires and Babies • by Katherine Garbera
Gabi De La Cruz thought she'd found Mr. Right...until he was arrested for murder! Now he's back and needs help with his young child, but is there room for a second chance when he's obsessed with clearing his name?

#2439 A SURPRISE FOR THE SHEIKH
Texas Cattleman's Club: Lies and Lullabies
by Sarah M. Anderson
Sheikh Rafe bin Saleed wants revenge, and he'll buy Royal, Texas, to get it. But will a night of unplanned passion with his enemy's sister give him a baby he didn't bargain for?

#2440 A BARGAIN WITH THE BOSS
Chicago Sons • by Barbara Dunlop
Playboy brother Tucker has no desire to run the family corporation, but a scandal forces his hand. His trial by fire heats up even more when he clashes with the feisty, sexy secretary who's hiding a big secret from him...

#2441 REUNITED WITH THE REBEL BILLIONAIRE
Bayou Billionaires • by Catherine Mann
After being ordered to reunite with his estranged wife to keep his career stable, a football superstar realizes that their fake relationship is more than an assignment. It might be what he wants more than anything else...

#2442 SECRET CHILD, ROYAL SCANDAL
The Sherdana Royals • by Cat Schield
Marrying his former lover to legitimize his secret son's claim to the throne becomes more challenging than prince Christian Alessandro expected. Because Noelle Dubonne makes a demand of her own—it's true love or nothing!

HDCNM0316

REQUEST YOUR FREE BOOKS!
2 FREE NOVELS PLUS 2 FREE GIFTS!

Ⓗ HARLEQUIN®

Desire

ALWAYS POWERFUL, PASSIONATE AND PROVOCATIVE

HDI5

Anna dropped the towel and unzipped the bag, staring at the contents with no small amount of horror. There was… underwear inside it. Underwear that Chase had purchased for her for their first fake date. She grabbed the pair of panties that were attached to a little hanger. Oh, they had no back. She supposed guessing her size didn't matter much. She swallowed hard, rubbing her thumb over the soft material. He would know exactly what she was wearing beneath the dress. Would know just how little that was.

He isn't going to think about it. Because he doesn't think about you that way.

He never had. He never would. She was never going to touch him, either. She'd made that decision a long time ago. For a lot of reasons that were as valid today as they had been the very first time he'd ever made her stomach jump when she looked at him.

She tugged on the clothes, having to do a pretty intense wiggle to get the slinky red dress up all the way before zipping it into place. She took a deep breath, turned around. She faced her reflection in the mirror full-on. She looked… Well, her hair was wet and straggly, and she looked half-drowned. She didn't look curvy, or shimmery, or delightful. She sighed heavily, trying to ignore the sinking feeling in her stomach.

Chase really was going to have to be a miracle worker in order to pull this off.

"Buck up," she said to herself.

So what was one more moment of feeling inadequate? Honestly, in the broad tapestry of her life it would barely register. She was never quite what was expected. She never quite fit. So why'd she expect that she was going to put on a sexy dress and suddenly be transformed into the kind of sex kitten she didn't even want to be?

She gritted her teeth, throwing open the bedroom door and walking into the room. "I hope you're happy," she said, flinging her arms wide. "You get what you get."

Chase, who had been completely silent upon her entry into the room, remained so. She glared at him. He wasn't saying anything. He was only staring. "Well?"

"It's nice," he said.

His voice sounded rough, and kind of thin.

"You're a liar."

"I'm not a liar."

"Are you satisfied?" she asked.

His jaw tensed, a muscle in his cheek ticking. "I guess you could say that."

Don't miss TAKE ME, COWBOY by USA TODAY bestselling author Maisey Yates available April 2016 wherever Harlequin® Desire books and ebooks are sold.

www.Harlequin.com

Whatever You're Into... Passionate Reads

Looking for more passionate reads from Harlequin®?
Fear not! Harlequin® Presents, Harlequin® Desire and
Harlequin® Blaze offer you irresistible romance stories
featuring powerful heroes.

♦HARLEQUIN *Presents.*

Do you want alpha males, decadent glamour and jet-set
lifestyles? Step into the sensational, sophisticated world of
Harlequin® Presents, where sinfully tempting heroes ignite a
fierce and wickedly irresistible passion!

♦HARLEQUIN *Desire*

Harlequin® Desire novels are powerful, passionate and
provocative contemporary romances set against a backdrop of
wealth, privilege and sweeping family saga. Alpha heroes with
a soft side meet strong-willed but vulnerable heroines amid a
dramatic world of divided loyalties, high-stakes conflict and
intense emotion.

♦HARLEQUIN *Blaze*

Harlequin® Blaze stories sizzle with strong heroines and
irresistible heroes playing the game of modern love and lust.
They're fun, sexy and always steamy.

Be sure to check out our full selection of books
within each series every month!

www.Harlequin.com